Return to Liberty Corners

By

Maggie Morgan

ISBN: 0-75962-613-8

This book is printed on acid free paper.

1stBooks - rev. 8/29/01

Dedicated to Mikhail Ann
who simply loved and approved of us all.

Preface

Following the publication of "Welcome to Liberty Corners" the author found herself even more deeply involved with the 'Cornerites'. Interesting 'ordinary' people who actually enjoy being ordinary so much that, with luck, they may never change.

"Return to Liberty Corners" is simply a day by day account about people you may already know (if the 'goodness and mercy spirits' the scripture promises have been pursuing you) or those you would like to meet. Their children and their pets, who could try the patience of a saint if one was available, and their method of coping with all the nitty, and sometimes gritty problems you hope to avoid. Offered as a pleasant oasis in a world grown harsh, her author-friend Dr. Alexander, the 'Sherlockian', suggests Corners is "a trip back to sanity".

Chapter 1

A NEW YEAR IN THE CORNERS

You may recall how we saw the old year out in Liberty Corners, with a friendly, rather snowy, farewell in the Village Square. Most of the older among us with just a little sigh. Perhaps regret at unfinished business, unresolved problems?

And I feel I must send a word of reassurance to you cat lovers; yes, we did finally locate Gert Ealy's irascible old cat gentleman, Flinders, after some anxious moments. Rather easily, actually; it took only a few dainty steps in that unknown substance called snow, to convince him that life in the outside world was not his cup of tea. So Gert's husband, Tom, was able to scoop him down from the lower branches of the scrub oak not far beyond their front door. Flinders, like his next door neighbor, Hazel Bernie, does not take to uneven treatment; howls of indignation and a scratched wrist were the only signs of gratitude he offered Tom.

Hospitality Week, our end of year community effort, had been a real success; the fourth year in a row! We are trying not to feel smug and self righteous. Judge Guyus would soon take the wind out of our sails on that point I'm afraid. But we are addicted to the fun of our concerted effort. Even the work involved gives us an opportunity, and an excuse, for extra visiting. Busy Alma Grant finds time to call on Marion Lozier, ostensibly for some fresh herbs, and the latest news of our project. Even Lilly Grigsby, who takes a rather dim view of the whole thing, has been seen to smile indulgently; while she bullies the enthusiastic *Fruit Cake Ladies* from United Methodist, to talk less, and nibble less of their supplies! The congratulations we receive from outlying communities is icing on the cake for the rest of us. We love it.

Now it's a brand new year. We are filled with brave intentions; mending our ways is our corporate goal and dedicated purpose. My friend Marion Lozier and I (I'm Miss Bloome from the bank you may remember) have agreed, with a skeptical laugh, that our enthusiasm on this subject may last till the end of the month. There are some among us who know we need to change though, believe me! I'm sure Lilly Grigsby has a fund of information on ways her husband Arthur might shape up. And, while Hazel Bernie lavishes most of her attentions and corrections on her rather past her prime daughter, Lila Mae, I have found her studying the rest of us with a disapproving eye when we gather at Village meetings. As for Judge Carpentar... Well, I'm sure we have never reached his dear departed wife's standards. I wonder if he ever let Beulah know how much value he placed on her cheerful outlook while she was still among us?

Our inimitable handyman's good intentions have already taken action. Crum has scraped the flaking lettering from the west side of his truck, making it even uglier than before, and plans to get rid of all the useless paraphernalia he has hauled around since the departure of his young wife Loretta. *She of the spike heels and crimson toe nails* that scandalized Hazel Bernie so. He plans to keep accurate records of his business activities he has assured everyone! We think Judge Carpentar has heen warning him about the I.R.S. breathing hot breaths down scrawny necks this year. So Crum has purchased a thick note pad at the Emporium, and a whole package of broad point pens. Those relegated to the bargain table.

****

After Christmas *Half Price* sales flourish everywhere. Having survived the pre-holiday shopping hassle, we vowed never to go through those horrors again. However, the second day following Christmas will probably find most of us cued in long lines outside our major stores. Those with bold signs on their windows offering *30% TO* 50% *Off All Name Brand Items.*

Young Trinity Blankenship (the not legally adopted but emotionally acquired *daughter* of the Ealy's), and her close friend Gloria, are near hysteria at the prospect of acquiring Designer Jeans at a price they can afford. At least Trinity feels she can afford, if she can wheedle Gert Ealy into a loan against next months allowance.

National Dry Goods in Bethany has had to set aside a whole section, in the rear, on the second floor of course; to accommodate the toys, clothing, gifts and shoes that did not meet with our approval, or our buying power, during the season. That the tables are placed to the store owners advantage is obvious. Our greed must traverse and resist the entire first floor, now resplendent with exciting new merchandise, to take advantage of the bargains so dear to our hearts.

The escalators carrying us all heavenward will be working overtime. Lila Mae Bernie will be hovering anxiously; her aging mother, Hazel, insists on moving at her own pace, regardless of the mechanical stairway. That she will hesitate one second too long and the escalator jaws will encapsulate her wavering foot is a horror we all have envisioned. But Hazel loves bargains as much as we do. Hoorah for Year End Sales!

Chapter 2
MOMENTS

The weeks following the holidays is almost traditionally a 'dull as ditch water' period, everywhere. And we are no exception. It seems we have exhausted all our enthusiasm on the time devoted to our Hospitality Week celebration, plus our own personal festivities. Forbidding weather promotes and excuses our lethargy; we are content to mark time indoors.

Clemmy Lukes, having done so well with sales of her beautiful quilts during our celebration week, is garnering yards of fabric for an even more ambitious project. She has had an order from a lady clear over in Mackinaw County for a *Grecian Star quilt.* A pattern she has never tried before. She is soliciting help from her enthusiastic niece Emmy, after school hours, for the tedious cutting of circles. Clemmy also made a killing in piece goods; when National Dry Goods staged their annual end 'of year clearance' sale.

The orphaned Luke children are enjoying every unsupervised hour at their disposal. That Auntie Clem has been forced to run a tight ship with her late start on motherhood we all recognize. She carries the load almost alone. Grandpa Lukes is a cheerful, rather unworldly old man, who spends more time and effort with God than with God's adopted children. Perhaps Ben has inherited the same spiritual *gene.* Surrounded by too many girls, he prospers in Gramp's company.

****

Hazel Bernie is chafing under house confinement. Inclement weather has closed what we call her observation post, in her side yard, for weeks now. The view from her window is very limited. Addie Larkin's swing hangs motionless; no sign yet of the hinges getting oiled, Addie's redoubtable son Edgar has never done anything interesting for the neighbors to enjoy or talk about; aside from his failure to buy another can of spray for the swing chains, that is. The one dollar investment; that both refuse to accept as a personal obligation, has kept mother and son at swords points for two years. And Hazel Bernie in a state of constant, but amused, irritation.

Next door, Gert Ealy's Flinders has shown complete feline disloyalty. He has no intention of leaving his post near the floor furnace during the day and the hearthstone evenings, for the icy world out there.

Little Charlie Lozier, Hazel's side kick, (and the innocent source, we think, of much Village information), has been forced to remain at home for the past week. Suffering from what Grandma Marion worries is a heavy cold. In reality his life proceeds pleasantly indeed; with delicious hot lemon drinks for his cough, (which must be summoned by force at strategic moments), chicken soup and hot biscuits on demand, and extra hours of T.V. allowed out of pity for his boredom. Boredom that was proving insupportable until his godmother, Gert Ealy, arrived with an armload of Comic books from the Emporium. Reverend Marcus has also paid a visit, bringing the printed Sunday School lesson Charlie missed last week. Marcus enjoyed a short rest with a cup of Marion's excellent coffee and a fresh cinnamon roll. Out of politeness he refused a second roll, so Marion has wrapped a half dozen in plastic wrap, to be stowed in a brown bag for his breakfast. After all, the poor man is alone, with no one to do for him but his sister-in-law Nettie; and that only when it suites her. Wouldn't it be lovely if he and Lila Mae Bernie found comfort in each others company?

In a fit of discontent Hazel Bernie mailed enquiries to several known resorts; those located in temperate climates, with the avowed intention of relocating. She has now spent many hours with the overflowing packet of highly colored catalogs and brochures that poor Purvis, the mailman, has dropped at the door. Every agency she contacted sent an enticing invitation to what presents itself as *Paradise;* invaluable properties seen in every clime except our own, at indescribably reasonable prices! Lila Mae, overcome with alarm as she faced the possible task of moving her Mama's elderly bones to a new and strange region, fled to Marcus Severn's study for consolation.

A timid knock on the closed door brought a reassuring "Come," and she pushed the door open; standing before the desk, thin hands twisting, eyes about to run over, she began an agitated recital.

"I'm sorry to disturb you Marcus, but it's Mama again. She's determined to leave the Corners. Says she can't stand this climate any more. Going to sell out and move to where there's sunshine all year. South or west, she isn't sure which. And... I can't reason with her... and oh... I can't leave the Corners..." Her voice ends in a wail and she is trembling.

Kindly Marcus, alarmed at the obvious anguish being visited upon kind, long suffering Lila Mae got up from his desk hurriedly. Almost unconsciously he put a protective arm about her shoulders and drawing her thin frame against his solid strength.

"Now Lila Mae, now Lila Mae," his voice consoled, "You know your Mama won't leave the Corners. Why it's been home to her all her life. Born right down the road, raised here, married here. Why she'd have to give up her house, built by her own husband all those years ago." He shook his head in complete disbelief.

"No, Lila Mae, knowing Hazel as long as I have I don't see her, at this time of her life leaving her home, all her friends..." Here he hesitated momentarily. Had Hazel Bernie, with her rather daunting outlook on life, managed to keep any deep friendships?

The moment of sustaining compassion passing he withdrew his supporting arms and stepped back from Lila Mae's palpable leaning. A more detached cheerfulness made itself heard. "You go back now and let your Mama read and enjoy all the colored brochures Purvis brings to the door." He hesitated and here his usual kindly expression assumed a rather crafty shading. "In fact, you read them too: share her enthusiasm, act excited about the whole idea." Lila Mae stared questioningly as he added, "It was our wise heavenly Father, remember, who advised us to 'agree with thine adversary quickly', to avoid disaster."

Following this serious conversation with Reverend Marcus Lila Mae began to camouflage her real concerns. She enthused over every possible location, encouraged every step toward a change of environment, decried every negative aspect and promised every help in the venture. Hazel was not pleased.

In fact she soon tired of the accumulation of paper, wondered why Lila Mae was full of silly notions about leaving the Corners. Was it mid-life crisis with Lila Mae?

Hazel decided instead to contact the painters from Minton, who would be working on Ivy's Mansion, for an estimate on the redoing of her own house.

****

Judge Carpentar has allowed the AWG's (our official Adult Walking Group) a brief respite after the holidays. Although he knows full well that the eating and drinking binge we have all indulged has had a disastrous affect on our already less than Greek-god figures. I think he has permitted us to enjoy this fleeting sense of freedom from tyranny because he knew he could not generate enough interest in keeping fit. We are concerned with plain survival, in snow, sleet, and wearying weather. With sidewalks to be shoveled, almost hourly, during the worst storms; furnaces to be dealt with, and cars to be eased from snow banked gutters daily. We hope he does not get mixed signals over these few missiles of watery sunshine that have been tossed our way.

After weeks of holiday goodies, with Marion Lozier's baked turkey with twice baked sweet potatoes, and two suppers featuring Texas Beef Soup, Gert Ealy has begun preaching diet and fitness to poor Tom, her husband, almost around the clock. It begins with breakfast of course. He is limited to one slice of toast and one soft boiled egg, with his uncreamed, unsweetened coffee. Or he can alternate with one bowl of Healthy Bran, with skim milk and his coffee.

That he has been witnessed perched on a stool at The Barn Door, almost immediately after he arrives at his office down in the Village, is common knowledge. That his order invariably includes a stack of pancakes, half a dozen sausage, and three eggs over easy, is also known. Thanks to Judy, our observant waitress.

Tom, after suggesting sweetly that Gert check to see if she has a Ministerial License in force, swears that a pulpit is his next home building project. With a comfortable pew for himself. Maybe he hopes to sleep through Gert's sermon. Gert intends to get his name on AWG's list even while snow still falls. Guyus Carpentar, viewing Tom's track record on exercise, is not optimistic. Some of us, already on Dr. Angus' overweight problem list, avoid any contact with Guyus. When we meet, warned by Charlie Lozier's giggling hiss "here come de judge" we, the cowardly, take another route home.

Chapter 3
INTERESTING CHANGES

It's only mid-January, the early spring thaw hasn't even set in yet, officially. But Richard Ivy has already hired Ed Beazley from Superior Contractors, over in Minton, for a complete make-over for the Mansion; inside and out. That their estimate was satisfactory we can only guess. We all have a private interest in the Superior Contracting Company; after all, the business was hatched down here in the Hollow, and we've watched Ed move his son and his daughter right into the action as soon as they were steady on their feet. The boy into construction and Babba into the office. Ed likes help, and family help is less expensive. When Tom Ealy, from Acme Realty, heard the figure the Beazleys quoted he suggested another estimate to Richard. Tom has a favorite that he deals with in Bethany. But Richard can get testy when it's a question of loyalty to our own...

Perhaps this will explain the truly mammoth clearing of his double city lot last year? That Richard had taken advantage of the unexpected clear spell, weather wise, directly after Christmas, to begin a serious cleanup job was noteworthy. His motivation is still not crystal clear however.

Due to the rumors of romance surrounding Richard and Miss Geraldine, senior librarian, we were all interested in anything and everything concerning the 'Mansion.' After all, the Ivy's have been one of our leading family's as far back as we can remember.

Superior Contractors, who advertise a fleet of trucks, (two pick ups and a van, to be exact) actually consists of Ed Beazley and his son and a crew of rather boisterous young painters and carpenters, all plugged in to the local radio station. They worked out of a two by four shack originally. That was before they installed several telephones and went big time on us. Most of us don't feel we can afford them now, but Richard, of course, suffers no pain in the pocket book. And they are good workers, artisans really, and Richard can afford the best.

In my cozy house on Main Street I have been able to watch the comings and goings of Ed Beazley, and the gangling Goochie. Goochie was given the civilized Christian name of Garth some twenty odd years ago but a family baby joke lingers on. There are to be no structural changes we understand. Cupola and delicate gingerbread trim are to remain intact, for which we are all thankful. After all, the century old Mansion is one of Liberty Corners showcase items, along with Richard's ornate Ivy Towers business building. Market House, equally dear to our hearts, is County property.

Frigid air is keeping all our doors closed so we can only guess at the Beazley's progress. But the sound of wrenching wood and hammer blows that resound from the kitchen area of the Mansion tells Marion Lozier, the gourmet chef next door, that the latest in cooking gadgetry is in store for some lucky woman. She is concerned that it is to be wasted on the one who prefers instant coffee and soda crackers! Has she heard the gossip about Miss Geraldine's diet.?

While we could only speculate about what Richard had in mind when he did all the landscaping last December, now we will settle in to watch. Geraldine, the senior librarian's reaction will be interesting. We are convinced she might be the reason behind the changes.

****

Marion Lozier lifted her starched curtain, careful not to disturb the fancy ruffled edge, and stared at the activity practically whirling about the Mansion. So early in the morning, so unusual in Liberty Corners quiet ambience. What in the world was that truck bringing in now; clear from where? Couldn't tell from the shape or the size really. She smiled ruefully; shame on me for such nosiness. Lowering the curtain she stepped back into the warm kitchen; her cheerful sunny haven. That smelled of pancake batter, and fresh berry syrup; with just a hint of the germicide she had used in the mop pail yesterday in her determined effort to thwart the childrens germ carrying talent.

Charlie, seated at the kitchen table lifted the syrup pitcher carefully. If he didn't clink against the edge of his plate, Gram, now running hot water into her dish pan, might not be aware that more black raspberries than pancakes were being eaten. He licked a blob of juice from the lip as he set the pitcher back in place. "Gram, you should have seen the trouble the men from Bethany Hardware had lifting that new refrigerator off the truck yesterday. It was so big... and both of those men were so short..." Just remembering made Charlie giggle.

Automatically Marion shook her head, "You shouldn't be minding the neighbors business honey. Shouldn't be watching everything that is going on at Ivy's. Richard hate's that."

"But Gram, everyone is."

"I know, I know. We're all guilty, but it's wrong. And how did you know it was a refrigerator, must have been in a carton of some kind..."

Charlie nodded a knowing head. "We didn't know for sure. It was big like a freezer or something, but we couldn't read the words on the box from on the wall, so Legs went over and asked Goochie, and he said..." Seeing another reprimand on the way Charlie hurried to avert. "Goochie doesn't mind if we bother him Gram, he really doesn't. His Daddy yells at him for wasting time, but Goochie likes to talk to us"

Marion turned the hot water an full force, and stacked her dishes in the rack. Charlie made a half hearted effort to remove a sticky smear from his chin with a dry paper napkin; was forced to dampen a corner in his water glass, (without spilling any on the breakfast cloth Gram just replaced yesterday) and pushed his chair back.

"Okay if I go find Legs, Gram? See if he wants to come over for the day?" And here he adds diplomatically, "And we won't watch the Ivy's today, Gram... Or at least, we won't ask Goochie any questions. Okay?"

Chapter 4

A FAMILIAR THEME-A NEW LOOK

The main subject of our conversations this month has been "What in the world has happened to our weather patterns?" Snuggled down as we are in the Corners, we have never actually participated in the horrendous conditions we witness on the evening news. Those things happened to *them,* but not to *us.* Not until now.

Richard Ivy's reconstruction project, looming large in our rather closed community, was brought almost to a standstill. Our usually beneficent climate has indulged in outrageous temper tantrums. Attacked with such ecstatic fury by early March winds, many of the ancient elms along Old McKinney Road fell victim, and made driving down that road what little Charlie Lozier mistakenly referred to as a real hizzard. *Hazard,* perhaps?

The big yellow County trucks, equipped with the latest mechanical munchers are moving purposefully down the thoroughfare; voracious beasts, pulling limbs, branches, twigs, and leaves into their waiting maws. A chewing, grinding sound resonates for miles as they digest the plant bounty. Marion says Charley wondered if they ever have to burp after their greedy guzzling.

Needless to say the County Fathers had to be urged into clearing action by almost hourly calls from Richard, and several irate letters from the desk of Judge Guyus.

With the road finally passable, the Beazley's will be able to defend their time schedule on the Mansion almost intact. Some days Goochie Beazley was hard pressed to keep four wheels on the same surface in his lighter van; hauling lumber during the downpours became a monumental task. The driver of the big rig insists he deserves a gold medal for his 'beyond the call of duty' efforts. Knowing the Beazley's tight accounting system I don't think he should hold his breath.

As to the rest of the Village, no one carries as big a stick as Richard. So none of Hazel Bernie's complaints went beyond the front desk at the county office. That the stretch of Edward Graham Road that faces her property is fast eroding into a serious stream bed is clear to the rest of us. But not to *them,* apparently. The River Jordan, fed from the downpour in surrounding hills, flowed by without hindrance. Fording left to the devises of home owners, with or without Gods intervention.

****

Apart from weather, the preparation for the Christmas 'DO' that we hold in such warm affection, is creeping into our corporate thinking. Our regular town meeting in the Richard Ivy wing of the Library, will be called the first of May. Everyone likes an early start on deliberations.

While Judge Carpentar still insists on a formal notice, posted on the bulletin board down at the *Morning Sun,* by April 15th, we have already 'cussed and discussed the whole issue and made our own preparations. I understand that Hazel Bernie had a list of changes she wanted made over our efforts of last year. What most of us felt was a very successful year.

****

Mr. Felson, truly beloved principal of Edward Graham Elementary, is determined to present a live show, featuring some of his most hopeful students. We are all interested and involved in the Corners children, so he won't find any opposition.

Since Kursty Lukes is the only one of Clemmy's grandchildren likely to be involved in Mr. Felson's production, some sibling rivalry may ensue. While Emmy and Poppy have no theatrical ambitions; and with Poppy, even the getting up in class to read aloud can be a sore trial. But to Ben, just a month short of celebrating another birthday, the possibility of appearing in Mr. Felson's play is interesting. Especially the part of Eyore.

Why were all the good things happening to girls? As the only Luke grandson he is beginning to feel hedged in by females; three sisters and an Aunt. That his obvious need for a large dog, all his own, has met with denial has been a sore point between himself and Auntie Clem. Even Gramps was cautious about giving his okay on this issue.

"Poor Clemmy has her hands full already Ben. I don't feel comfortable adding a dog to her schedule. Yes," he interrupted the promises that were about to pour forth, "I know you mean to take care of it yourself, but..."

Having already raised two sons Gramps tends to be skeptical. The fact that Poppy has not been allowed to replace the cocker puppy that was puppy-knapped from the yard last year did not ease Bens sense of injustice. (The same cocker puppy who invaded closets to make a steady diet of tennis shoes, shoe laces, clothing that was supposed to be deposited in hampers, etc.etc.) The raucous little bundle of nervous energy and fun still mourned by all.

****

Our last meeting at the library did not produce any genuine surprises, except that we were made very aware that the Market House was either shrinking in size, or we were increasing in the number of people needing space to exhibit. Crum, our all important village helper, and solver of problems no one else wants to handle, came up with a suggestion even Judge Guyus listened to. Didn't give immediate approval to, you understand, but listened. Handsome graying head on one side, questioning look on his face; why hadn't he been approached personally about this idea before it was brought to the attention of the ordinary folk? Had Crum already talked this over with Richard, and why hadn't he been consulted? Crum, who insists on maintaining a low profile, (from the last seat in the last row) simply suggested that, instead of violating the present structure, why not borrow the moneys accumulated in the Liberty Corners

Crises Fund and build a replica of the present structure? *Not a newer, later version* he hurried to assure us; heaven forbid that we erase our historical identity as most of America has done; but a genuine copy. Maybe at the other end of the Village?

Marcus Severn's head was nodding in approval before the last words were out; and I believe Clarence Crum had earned an honorary degree from Miss Campbell, the American history buff from Liberty College, before he took his seat.

Coffee cups replenished, and double chocolate brownies offered all around, (who baked these super size goodies?) we prepared to disband. Another hurdle conquered... or another conflict induced?

Chapter 5

SUNDAYS & HOLIDAYS

The days of February are bringing on a restless expectancy in the Village. Even though the weather is still harsh, with feathery snow greeting us early mornings only to disappear as the first pale sunlight breaks through. The road leading out to Old Farm, which is a general favorite for all our walkers, is still stark and uncompromising. Even late Sunday morning may find it deserted of foot traffic, except for poor Mr. Wilfred, editor of *The Morning Sun.* Perhaps he prefers privacy for his tortoise like constitutional on damaged legs?

Spring juices are rising in humans however, and the Grants, third generation owners of Old Farm, are making extra demands on Manuel the Mexican helpers time. Alma, for her own special gardens, and Ebert for the never ending farm needs.

While Ebert has earned fame with his extraordinary greenhouse results, Alma has captured our hearts and taste buds each summer with monster strawberries, giant size red and black raspberries, and prize winning rhubarb. This latter, almost an obsolete item in markets across the country, has become one of her biggest successes. Old Henry Lockwood from Lockwood's Family Market in Cameron drives over almost daily when Alma's rhubarb crop comes in. Fresh baked rhubarb pie is still a prime favorite at The Barn Door as well as among Corners housewives.

Ebert takes advantage of Alma's success. In season the largest leaves are wrapped about the loaves of fresh churned butter we still beg for. Two pound loaves, in oiled wrapping paper (still stamped with Ebert's own trade mark) trickles of milk oozing from their cold sides, to seep into the odds and ends of padding provided by knowledgeable drivers on rear floors of cars. Buyers are from as far away as Bethany. A product not to be found anywhere but in Liberty Corners we assume.

"With major producers taking over the dairy industry, "Ebert keeps reminding us," this catering to personal cranky appetites is a finished, done, past redemption extra. Don't count on even one more year!"

We listen to his tirade and nod humbly. But Friday afternoons and the week ends before holidays will find Alma's driveway lined with cars of hopeful cranks.

****

The marching band from Liberty High is beginning to practice now that the heaviest weather is past (we hope). After at least two hours indoors with their instruments, they line up on the somewhat muddy, and often slushy tarmac of the parking lot to coordinate their steps.

As the tallest member, and also the most controlled, Martin Grant brings up the rear with sober, careful timing. Perhaps, as an aftermath of his miraculous healing, Martin is still not entirely adjoined to *this world* and it's disjointed chaos. At any rate he adds a degree of stability to a group that can get out of hand at the slightest provocation. The mannerisms of Mr. Hamilton the band master; the abrasiveness of Richard Ivy, who takes a heavy handed interest. (He provides all the financial support for those wonderful trips outside the county, when we compete with bands from Cameron, Bethany and Minton.) All come under humorous attack. That the young consider everything past thirty primordial we understand, having been there.

****

With two Presidents Birthdays and Valentines Day to celebrate in February, and Ash Wednesday to be observed, academic curriculum is falling on hard times. Much to the children's joy. All Districts may not operate on the same liberated schedule as ours, but the attention span is definitely in peril at Edward Graham Elementary and Liberty High. The young push their luck in a more relaxed atmosphere.

****

While years have passed, some of the old customs still cling to us. So, the approach of Valentines Day finds the youngest Luke children spending a great deal of their after school hours at the dining room table. Surrounded by masses of red tissue paper, yards of paper lace, and dobs of glue. A bygone pleasure is being revived; how the glue finds it's way into Kursty's braids despite Clem's constant reminding is a mystery that never gets solved.

Emmy Lou, at eleven, is spending time, and her rather limited savings, at Stones Drug Store. She is finding that the twenty-five cents weekly allowance that Grandpa Lukes offered with a grand flourish on her tenth birthday is buying less and less. They have just put in a whole counter of Valentine cards at Stone's; suddenly she feels too sophisticated and worldly to indulge in the home made variety; even while she offers advice to the sibling and fingers the bits and pieces of trim on the table enviously.

A Valentine fit for Polly's favorite male teacher can create a family crisis, which Ben finds hilarious. After being kidded by schoolmates concerning an avowal of love by fourth grader Agnes Potts, Ben is developing a belligerent attitude about girls in general, and Agnes in particular. Out of Aunt Clemmy's hearing he has threatened to "knock Agnes into the middle of next week" if she sends him a Valentine. A threat that has added a great deal of excitement to Kursty's concept of true love.

****

Today the sun is actually out in full dress. Even though the snow that engulfed us since New Years is still piled along the sidewalks and gutters in rather nasty gray patches. The blemished mixture under hedges is melting and the unexpected warmth has sent puny rivulets of water slithering along the sidewalks. We must step carefully. The lowered temperatures predicted on the six o'clock news will reverse all this of course. The magician who turned ice to water by noon, will reverse his decision before dark. But for the moment the euphoria of this unexpected token of approaching spring is engulfing us.

We are feasting our eyes and our ears on the calming hush of Sunday. Main Street stretches itself regally for it's full four blocks. The only clots of color are outside the Emporium Market, where Albert Hastings has given such care to window boxes full of artificial flowers.

Which some find ludicrous, but they relieve our eyes from the somber palette that stretches before us during the winter months. Those two large flowering shrubs in pots on either side of the glass doors (surrounded by wire, as unleashed dogs have wreaked havoc once before) have recovered from their snow blanket and are none the worse.

My tidy house, nestled between the old Grover place and the empty lot Acme Reality has been trying to sell me for the past ten years (I'm Miss Bloome from the bank) usually makes a colorful display with an arch of roses over the trellised gate. Today it is a somber study in white and grayed green. All my mothers ancient rose collection, still thriving under Manuel's direction, will sleep until May's sunshine awakens them.

The only foot traffic is a little group of the elderly who are just exiting Methodist Church after service. With sidewalks clear of snow they will enjoy a brisk but careful walk home for a solid Sunday lunch. Very tender roast beef, mashed potatoes and brown gravy; followed perhaps by a wintertime favorite, homemade coconut cream pie. Or apple cobbler with clotted cream if you were lucky enough to be asked to dinner out at Grant's Old Farm. All foods prime suspects on Dr. Angus's list of no, no's. While the young, with their full set of natural teeth consume endless salads and crunchy roughage, we, the over sixties, have reverted to our childhood favorites.

****

For many years now nearby towns have followed the lead of big cities and maintained a steady commercial hum in their business sections, from dawn to dark: daily, holidays, and Sundays. The clink of shekels passing freely from hand to outstretched hand even as the Church bells peal an urgent Christian message. Not so in the Corners. At the odd times when Reverend Marcus has been forced to be in Bethany during church hours, his sister-in-law vows he carries a scourge in a small bag behind the drivers seat. Doubtless with the hope that someday he will be called by the Almighty to chase money changers from even the neighborhood of the temple.

Mumblings and grumblings on a minor scale concerning the closed doors on Sunday may occur around holidays. Iva Cully could probably sell a few antiques to the wandering tribes from Bethany and Minton as they drive aimlessly on weekends. But for the most part we are satisfied to earn our bread from nine to five all week. Until ten on Saturdays for the Emporium and The Barn Door, of course. There are no stringent laws controlling our hours actually, we just do what has always worked for us.

Monday will bring on a brisker pace. Not the harsh drive of the city, but Albert Hastings will open the big doors and lower the awning at the front of the Emporium by eight o'clock. We will begin to gather early, as bread usually ends in short supply for many of us after the week end. Yetta Wiley and Alma Grant will doubtless have their bread machines busy on their behalf, but the remainder of us will hope the bread truck from Bethany has arrived promptly with our fresh loaves. Arthur Grigsby would have enjoyed the last can of his beer Sunday night, and must replenish. So, we gather for physical food, and yes... the latest village news.

Chapter 6
VILLAGE TALK

The news that Noel Carpentar had approached Cogswald and Bender, the Real Estate people from Bethany, about that acreage on the hillside just south of the College has become official. It's a lovely, partially level parcel, and would make a good homesite. With plenty of room for children to roam about. And even a small stable, if the owner was so inclined.

Arthur Grigsby was sure that is what was under consideration when he saw Noel's red convertible parked off the road, and Noel walking arm in arm, with old Bender, over the length of the property this past weekend. Lilly has her doubts. At an arthritic seventy five George Bender is still active in the business we know, but walking uphill to that site with just the possibility of a sale?

Hazel Bernie had her own opinion. She went to school with George Bender at Edward Graham Elementary, and she's convinced he would pull his arthritic back up a mountain if there was a dollar on the other side. To her, old George sails near the wind.

Marion's hopes were raised by the news. With the money he inherited from his mother Noel will be able to make serious plans. It would be so wonderful if he would marry that nice Cordelia Wiley and have a big family. His father, Guyus, had been too career minded; had waited far too long before he proposed to Beulah Graham. One lone chick was the result. With Marion, having had three, her grandson Charlie is a constant reminder of the loneliness of only children.

I will have to admit that Noel Carpentar's purchase of the lovely eight acre sight was known to me from the start. While I am no longer active at Interstate Bank, George Bender and I made many a deal while I served as Loan Officer. And we still have friendly contact at the Main Office in Bethany. Cogswald and Bender do all their business with the Main Branch of course. George Bender has never been close mouthed when it's someone we both know; news seeping from floor boards again? With Noel's inheritance; (Beulah Graham was the only child of old Edward Graham and heir to all his money) he was able to make a very sizable down payment on the property. That he is very excited and happy about his investment is obvious. His smile, always wide, has grown even wider. His obvious pursuit of the junior librarian is engaging our attention.

A true son of affable Beulah Graham Carpentar, easy going Noel is sharing his joy with all of us. Perhaps we will have one more family dynasty relatively secure. We are big on family dynastys in this area. Bethany has its Millikens and Akins, and Cameron has long been a Lockwood stronghold. With this outbreak of romance; Richard and Geraldine lower key, but all the more interesting really, (we feel Richard deserves another chance at happiness); if he will take it! Maybe we want some higher power to repay him for all the good he has bestowed on the village. Like uniforms for the teams, buildings the county wouldn't finance, etc. etc. We are experiencing a benevolent period worthy of Reverend Marcus Severns most innovative sermons.

At fifteen, Martin Grant, the budding author and Professor Carpentar worshiper, views adult romance as a modern day Egyptian plague, and is discountenanced to discover the feet of his idol turning to clay.

Across the Village Pastor Severns views the whole business as none of anyone's business and is reminding us once more "Let your communication be yea, yea; nay nay. Anything more comes of evil." And until he is told of definite wedding plans he refuses to speculate. That Noel will choose to be married in the same church that witnessed the rather elaborate ceremony of Judge Nathan Carpentar's son Guyus to Beulah Graham some thirty five years ago he has no proof.

Chapter 7
TAXES

March is not a favorite month with most of us in Liberty Corners. Still too reminiscent of a harsh winter, and not beneficent enough to tantalize us with the sweet promises of spring. And...we will have to face Tax Forms; Itemized Deductions; and in Marion Lozier's case, Judge Carpentar and his ominous predictions. Seated at her dining room table, pencil in hand, a yellow tablet spread before her, she took a rather near sighted look out the street side windows. The only windows that face directly out on Old McKinney Road. They afford the only newsworthy items on this dreary March day.

Having roared in like a lion, scattering doorstep carpets clear to the road, and almost tearing Charlie's shirts and trousers from the wash line, March has now plumped down to a sullen gloom. Piles of leaves, left over from a beautiful fall display, are still heaped in drab disarray against the hen coop and the garage door. The garage has become her personal catch-all. Now she sighed. Have to see if Crum had any time left over for simple gardening chores. Probably not, with his involvement in the restoration of the Mansion. While Ed Beazley and his son were actually in charge Richard still sets a great deal of store on Crum's opinions; and accepts, albeit grudgingly, Crum's simple advice. Crum, and his Daddy before him, have been looking over our shoulders all these years, giving us wise directions on almost every project we undertake.

Marion retrieved the yellow pad that was trying to lose itself under the pile of mismatched bills and statements; wishful thinking, the losing that is? After letting the months of January and February go by without getting her income tax records together, she is reaching the edge of the panic season. Judge Guyus, here she corrected her thinking, ex-Judge Guyus, was already glaring at her over his bifocals when they meet at the

Emporium. Each year he offers to see her through Tax Time Terror, and each year she reluctantly accepts his offer. Knowing, that by the fifteenth of April, their lifelong friendship would be in tatters and shreds. Laid back Marion is not an organized business woman. Marion is not truly organized in any area of her life. And to Guyus Carpentar, disorder is the red flag that is waved before a bull. A large red flag, literally brushing against the steaming nostrils of an infuriated bison.

The first words of greeting between Marion and her benefactor are guaranteed to be, "Got your paper work tidy and complete, have you; haven't forgotten to list the expenses for your business venture; kept all your receipts and an accurate sales record I assume?"

His steely gray eyes assure her that he is far too smart to assume any such a thing, in her case, and pin her shrinking soul to the mast. At that moment she admits she wouldn't even remember where she had stashed the sales book. That it was the day after she discovered Charlie and Pedro had made free use of the bare pages following her last entries, she did recall. The pages they had used for their latest scout rules. Having been warned by Tom Ealy, in ringing tones, to "List in a safe place for future reference".

A tearful confrontation with Marion over the misuse of her valuable sales record book brought out the explanation that Charlie was sure the red notebook that Marion seemed to guard with her life was "the safest place in the world for the scout rules Gram."

****

Taxation I'm afraid, brings out the very worst in all of us. Hazel Bernie is what Crum refers to as, "not a bad old soul," but presents a real lesson in tax resistance and opposition. She falls only a little short of the delinquent payment syndrome. Maybe you remember the year metal buttons appeared on the market, stating, `I'm Joining The Tax Revolt.' Hazel ordered a dozen. She still wears hers like a badge of honor.

But since Charlie Lozier considers Hazel his special friend, she can't be all bad. She does keep up her property out there on Edward Graham Road. That nice white clapboard that Aaron Bernie built some forty odd years ago. But the County and Hazel have never been on friendly terms at any time of the year, certainly not around the fifteenth of April. She does pay her taxes. Oh my, yes; she does pay her taxes...

Denied access to the ear of the present reprehensible commissioner, (he's 'not at his desk' when she calls); some poor underpaid county employee gets an ear full the day Hazel receives what she perceives as a spurious, unwarranted tax statement. And yet again, on the day she sends in what she considers her 'taxation without representation' payment.

We all agree that the ditch that separates her front gate from the unpaved secondary road, remains unfilled, from time immemorial. And *they* have yet to part the waters when it's necessary to cross. That Addie Larkin's property to the west shares the same problem we know. Addie and her son Edgar ford the stream via a very unstable plank Edgar retrieved from Grandpa Luke's barn, and continue their uneventful journey through life. But every year, we, and the county, and the current county commissioner, are all made aware that Hazel Bernie pays taxes.

With the April fifteenth deadline staring us in the face, most of us in the Corners toe the mark, and have our forms completed and mailed by the first. Even sending our payments in early, if there is a possibility of a refund, oh happy day! Judge Carpentar has been able to secure a small, legitimate refund for Marion for several years, as her dwindling income reached the 'bottom of the barrel' status. We doubt that the sale of her herbs will have much impact on her earnings yet. She has not taken an ad in the county news, so she is strictly local so far. That the government will wait until we are beside ourselves before mailing the refund check is gospel.

Fortunately, having shared our common misery about money matters for several weeks, and argued. the wisdom of paying taxes *early* and letting *them* gain unearned interest on *our* money, we will take on a more cheerful attitude. Most of us will begin almost automatically to anticipate something constructive. Something happy? The Christmas 'Do'?

Still months away, not even to the actual planning stage yet, but Judge Guyus will begin to sound out Richard's opinions as they share coffee at the Barn Door before leaving for another day in their offices down in the Village. He is still very actively involved with all our decisions. Sometimes more than we might want.

Chapter 8
INCIDENTS

A small community can vibrate like the quills on a fretful porcupine, over what may appear to some as minor issues. Now the loss of one member of our extended family is causing us to draw together. To comfort each other in our loss, or to fortify ourselves against that ancient enemy, death? We aren't sure.

This week we are adjusting to the fact that old Mr. Worley will no longer be attending, or (according to how you viewed the situation) disrupting town meetings. Not that he constituted a genuine problem to any of us. Just a fringe irritation as he turned his hearing aid too low and required endless repetition of each suggestion made. That he was beginning to make inroads into Richard Ivy's store of patience we had noticed, every time we got together. However, we must consider now where we can find another such generous donor to all College projects; another willing volunteer for the endless fund raising for College sports programs; and yet another rather authoritative voice when we approach *them* about a County project. Richard and Guyus are our mainstays in that area, but after all, Joshua Worley was Liberty College for some thirty *y*ears.

But his death has left more of a genuine fracture in our village patchwork covering than we were initially aware. We did tend to 'look after' him. Almost always against his stubborn will, I might add. Marion's cooking was the only unqualified success when he fell into our hands. That the rest of us were hopeless amateur we were made aware.

Poor Miss Geraldine found out the hard way the day she brought him a rather lop sided loaf of whole wheat bread, fresh from her 'never before used' bread machine. His rather rancorous gratitude included the fact that his "uppers couldn't break through the outer shell and his lowers slipped dangerously over the inner limp." On re-reading the recipe, she discovered that she had used regular flour instead of the stipulated bread flour, and had measured her butter with too lavish a hand. The Circle of Love will continue, short of one almost full time recipient.

Frankly, he will be missed most grievously in the soliciting area. Always a sparse little contingent of rather unwilling volunteers; Mr. Worley, with his no nonsense approach was an outstanding success. It took quite a little courage to refuse his demands for donations, following his scholarly explanation of your civic duty. Cringe you might, but give you would.

Judge Guyus must unscramble the mounds of paper work that Joshua Worley has left behind. Instructions to those distant relatives whom we never cast eyes on in time of need. The same ones who received the Fruit Cake Ladies annual bounty. Guyus observes the rules of privacy meticulously; but a little hint that Mr.Worley had mixed emotions concerning one Albert Petry, his nephew by marriage, twice removed; and a Miss Amy Worley, address unknown, has surfaced. Designated Executor on two of the documents, Albert slipped into disrepute last year when he contemplated remarriage, after only ten yeas mourning for Mr. Worley's favorite niece. That Miss Amy Worley committed an equally heinous crime is obvious as her bequest gradually dimmed from a sound ten thousand dollars to a lackluster one thousand.

Liberty College is to be principle beneficiary. We expected that. The College has been Mr. Worley's whole life. Guyus will get it all straightened out. He has been un-muddling all our muddles for these past forty years, and while we may object, silently, to his methods, we do appreciate his expertise.

****

Sitting comfortably at Marion's kitchen table, coffee cups brimming, Gert Ealy and Marion have covered all the main points of the late Mr. Worley's passing.

"He was a nice old gentleman. Used to be quite friendly when we met at the market, although I wasn't sure he ever actually knew who I was." Marion smiled. "Once he began needing help from the Circle though, he recognized me. When he'd call he'd insist he wanted the raspberry syrup lady. What a way to be known!"

Gert shook her head. "He probably also remembered that you listened so patiently to his memories of Liberty College days. Bless his heart he loved to relive the past. I'm afraid he stopped living the day he turned sixty five and had to retire" she sighed. "Let's not fall into that trap Marion, okay? Let's get our act together now, and plan to *LIVE* until we actually do leave this world!" Gert's sanguine intensity always entertains Marion, even while she agrees in principle.

****

Some in the Corners have taken to physical exercise with an almost religious zeal. Now that the weather is being more cooperative, less threatening at least, McKinney Road is never without at least two or more cyclists. They move in a steady, determined pattern that speaks more of body building than pleasure. With heads down, enveloped in prescribed gear, a stranger might not recognize Noel Carpentar in his red racing jacket at the head of any group; or Marcus Severns, a little slower, but steady, in his usual conservative gray; or Mr. Wilfred slower yet, and usually riding alone at his own meditative pace. An abreviated journey that will end out at the highway. Round trip will average four miles or less.

We, the sluggards, will be content with walking to the Emporium when we are forced to, or a leisurely hike to Grants Farm when the wonderful spring weather begs us to come out. Lilly and Arthur Grigsby will even forego that simple form of exertion, as their hips are beginning to testify.

Chapter 9
SHARED WORRIES

Cordelia Wiley chose a small crunchy roll from the basket being offered by the waitress. An oriental, child size waitress, with a more than average interest in *who* she was serving. A conspiratorial smile said that her eyes had already recognized the man seated across the table. Recognized, and approved. When Noel hesitated in his choice of a roll she turned her little serving basket to the side piled higher, and urged yet a second roll. Cordelia grinned across at Noel and shook her head. Corner matchmaking was in full swing.

That Catagonia's culinary arts rate even higher than the Barn Door's according to Geraldine Cordelia questioned, as she held the luscious toasted morsel closer. A large dollop of fresh butter from Grant's Farms, and the clear danger of another inch of waistline... or restraint? She reached for her butter knife even as Noel attacked his second roll and began to enjoy his dinner.

"When we leave here we've got to go out and check our property again," Noel announced between bites." See how the view changes, day to night; and if more acreage is needed on the south side. There's another tract available next to ours", I can buy it if you like. And you really do like that piece of ground Cordy, don't you? I mean you really would like living up there?"

Purposely overlooking the stress he was placing on the personal pronouns, Cordelia began to laugh even while she raised a restraining hand.

"No, please, for heavens sake not again today! You already have everyone in the Corners laughing at us, with your 'new land owners' enthusiasm. Almost everyone that is. Hazel Bernie warns that you should check with the county about the latest tax program; scheduled for next year if the bill passes, and she's sure it will; before you invest in any more land. And Crum wonders if you know about the water problems they may have up on the hill?"

Ignoring future problems of increased taxes or decreased water supplies Noel continued, in a serious tone. "After we take another look I wish we could stop by over on McKinney Road. We really do need to talk to Guyus, make some kind of a formal announcement maybe?... After all he is my father, much as I hated to admit it when I was young. Who wants to be related to a Judge, for heavens sake. While some of your friends may be busy breaking the law? But, I know he's waiting. Not asking any questions, which is a nine day wonder. Probably hoping to avoid one of our 'confrontations.' That's the term he always used for what I called 'knock-down, drag-out fights,'" he recalled with a grin.

"He is aware of my intentions, of course. Our local spy network has recorded every trip to the library. And what those little volunteers didn't see..."

"They guessed or hoped," Cordelia added "'Nothing hidden that shall not be revealed' as Marcus guarantees." She laughed, "Do you suppose the Lord had Liberty Corners on His mind when He said that?"

"Yes, had to... But I know Guyus is beginning to feel out of it, with Mom being gone. And I know how much he would appreciate a personal visit with you, really get to know you, better than on the casual village friendship level."

He would have continued speaking, but he saw the change in Cordelia's whole manner. She lowered her fork slowly, and sat up. The warm tender alchemy of the past hour turned to silence. His own dear Cordy momentarily assumed the guise of the uncertain, and still rather uncommitted, librarian.

Cordelia was forced to realize that while Noel's tone rang with his usual confidence, his crooked grin was begging for reassurance. For a commitment that she couldn't bring herself to offer, even while she blamed herself. What was she doing? This dear man was offering her his love, his future, and everything she was supposed to want, and was she still letting her fears and doubts rule her life?

With yet another roll suspended in mid-air Noel stared at Cordelia. "Cordy darling, what's the matter? You aren't having second, or third, or fourth thoughts again?" he almost groaned.

Cordelia shook her head, upset by his intensity. "I'm afraid I'm already past the dozen mark Noel dear. Pro's and con's concerning our whole relationship... aside from friendship that is."

With tears already welling, she raised a restraining hand. "Not concerning my feelings for you, dear, dear Noel. That won't change, ever!"

"Then what in the world?"

Simple, uncomplicated Noel waited in unbelief for her explanation; his mind replayed a stirring scene; that first walk in the rain outside the College, in full view of moving but curious students; the moment that followed Cordelia's realization, probably for the first time, of what was happening between popular, sanguine Professor Carpentar and the cool impersonal librarian. Recognition, followed almost immediately by an emotional response; her damp raincoat pressed against his side, warm, unresisting fingers held tightly in his own, an expectant, adoring face held against his own for one brief moment.

Back in the familiar classroom some minutes later, his mind refused to concentrate on the proper use of the apostrophe. Cordelia's unrestrained reaction held him spellbound 'till the last class closed... But not total acceptance?

Cordelia marshaled her mental arguments, as the little waitress arrived with the second course. Forced to silence for the moment, Noel stretched to capture Cordelia's hand as the dishes were exchanged.

Dear, darling muddled Cordy. His mother would have loved this girl!

****

Marion, seated at her dining room window, pushed the lacy ruffle of her friendly criss-cross curtains aside for a better view of the street. The curtains that were due for a careful hand washing before summer was in full force. Would they last another year? She doubted it. Her attention wandered. Early hours, no one up and walking about yet.

With the deepest shrubbery and densest trees removed from Ivy's property she was able to get a clearer view of the Judge's door beyond. White iron scroll work of the guard door sharp and clear against the muted grays of the rather formal structure. Marion smiled as she analyzed the Judge to herself. Immeasurably helpful in legal matters, extremely impatient with all village stupidities, and yet always incredibly civil and correct when we approached him on any issue. But without Beulah's mitigating good humor and bonhomie even the house itself presented an 'at arms length' welcome.

Marion's perpetual worry bug wondered what the Judge would do, left alone in that quiet house, when Noel finally convinced Cordelia to marry him? That he would convince Cordelia the village was sure. The acquiring of that lovely property on the hill by Noel was all they had needed as a warranty of Noel's intentions. Much as he loved Guyus, surely he would not ask gentle Cordelia to live, even temporarily, in the Judge's awesome presence?

It would all work itself out... Marion shifted her attention to the present. The Grandfather Clock in the hall would be bonging out the seventh hour momentarily and that would bring Noel out of the house for his run along Nappy river. Such a nice young man: more like his mother every day. Much as she prayed for his marriage and happiness she would miss his daily run, his friendly greeting. Even Ivy's old dog Dracula would miss the pat on the head as Noel trotted by the front gate. Personal notice did not come Dracula's way that often, and while Charlie, short of stature took extreme exception to Dracula's artless greetings, "Gram, his tongue spits all over my face and neck! And he doesn't obey Gram. Even when I scold him and try to scare him away!" Noel did not seem to mind the moist kisses Dracula bestowed on his hands and legs.

A stirring in the bedroom overhead alerted her that Charlie was awake and ready for a new day of adventure. Maybe she could interest him and the amiable Pedro in helping Crum empty and reorganize the garage. Hopefully they would find a few things that Charlie, not to mention Marion herself, could bare to part with, and make room for new findings! Another of First Christian's White Elephant Sales must be in the offing wasn't it?

Chapter 10
PERSONALITIES

Gert Ealy is convinced there is a school hidden somewhere in Bethany, or perhaps Minton, that offers a degree in HOW TO BECOME A FIRST CLASS MARTYR. That Lilly Grigsby and Lila Mae Bernie have either graduated cum laud, or are at least enrolled, she is sure. She doubts that either one is a 'burning at the stake' candidate yet, but Lily at least, appears to be reaching the 'facing the lion' stage.

Arthur Grigsby is actually thinking about making an offer for that old property just beyond the Post Office. That ramshackle log building, dating back to who knows when, to be filled with the collectables that he means to accumulate, piece meal, from surrounding farms and villages. He refuses to believe that antique dealers from out of state have gleaned all the countryside for decades; leaving nothing for widows and strangers despite Biblical injunction.

Lily can just see herself compassed about for endless months, by germ ridden, and perhaps bug infested, cast offs. Remember the collection she lived with in her basement before the White Elephant sale last year?

****

Gert's Martyr theories have erupted again, as the Village discusses the possibility of an eighty-fifth anniversary celebration for our own United Methodist Church. That Lila Mae, First Christian's mainstay, would be that deeply involved in another denominations anniversary might be unfathomable any place, except in the Corners. Gert is still shaking her head in disbelief. Marion can't help laughing at Gert's outspoken comment, even while she defends Lila Mae.

"Lila Mae loves to serve, Gert. Her whole soul is involved with serving the Lord, in any Church, in. any capacity. And this sounds like an exciting project. Imagine, United M.E. has been calling the faithful to worship for almost eighty five years." She smiled, "It sounds so interesting that I'm thinking of offering some of my time, if I can be of any help. If I know you, you'll be doing something too."

Gert gave a humorous grimace. "You've found a day that has more than twenty four hours in it I assume? Charlie, and a growing business in herbs, and The Circle of Love, plus personal involvements must cover at least eighteen. Or are you one of those scientific wonders that I'm hearing about who don't require sleep? No thanks, you enjoy. All I need is one more project and Tom will leave home for sure."

Dismissing the whole idea, Gert took off for another busy day at the Art Center.

****

It was panic time up on Edward Graham Road this morning. Well, that's probably an exagerration, We don't generally indulge in as intense an emotion as that. But Hazel Bernie has been transferred once again to Bethany General Hospital. Faithful Grace Ealy, in her faithful station wagon, arrived in minutes after Lila Mae's frantic call. Grace said she could hardly understand Lila Mae's message, punctuated as it was, with sobs and hand wringing that she swears she could hear over the phone. But she took no chances and hurried to the rescue.

Hazel was indeed in some sort of a seizure. With breath coming in gasps, and an alarming shade of green-white on her parchment skin. She was still insisting that she could handle this herself, and "would not fall into the hands of that Dr. again." Hazel has never forgiven poor Dr. Angus for sending her to Bethany General last year against her better judgment. And Dr. has never forgiven her for leaving without his consent.

Lila Mae may be daunted after so many years of Hazel's tyranny, but Grace Ealy, after twenty years of teaching adolescents and coping with teen rebellion, is a no nonsense type. She and her lovely station wagon answer the call, whoever calls, and gets the job done. She told us she simply bundled the child size Hazel into the Missionary Quilt, ordered Lila Mae to get her necessary 'things' and headed for the door. Grace admitted the air was almost blue with Hazel's denunciations, but she was deposited safely in the wagon, and the journey began.

Dr. Angus arrived at Bethany General shortly and has taken charge with an iron hand. All in charge have strict orders: this time Hazel is to remain incommunicado, if necessary, until Dr. Angus releases her. While Hazel has diagnosed her own illness as "bird flu" Dr has serious doubts whether this is the actual disease. Maybe a bad case of T.V. infection from watching all the daily news casts? However, at well past eighty, according to Lila Mae, or the eighty even Hazel admits to, no chance can be taken. Hazel will be under observation until further notice.

With her Mama settled in the isolation ward Lila Mae has taken refuge in the silence of Graham Road. We will all check on Dr. Angus findings. Speculation is already rife as to how we are to cope with this 'foreign germ' invasion.

Marion Lozier's immediate concern was for Charlie of course. Charlie still spends much of his free time with his friend Mrs. Bernie and her famous spy glass. What germs did he come in contact with? Mrs. Gillies is advocating the immediate closing of all our borders, against all of what she terms "satanic spirits of disease." Did bird flu travel the same mysterious route to our door as the Hong Kong variety a few years back? And what type of lock or gate is required to repel a spirit germ?

Lila Mae will make her way to the church office for consolation. Reverend Severns, who is on intimate terms with the Almighty, makes no room for the devil and his works.

Chapter 11
THE LETTER

Word has just been received from Trinity Blankenship's long lost, and somewhat forgotten, parents. Lost so far as limited, official, investigation has been able to uncover, and perhaps purposefully forgotten by some. Usually, spurred on by anxious relative inquiries, missing persons reports receive immediate attention. Here however, we have the missing persons, but are missing the anxious relatives I'm afraid.

Gert has had a badly written note, penciled by Hettie Blankenship we assume, in a large childish scrawl, and stuffed in an envelope hearing the Bethany Dry Cleaner's emblem. Purvis, delivering mail, late as usual, took time to decipher the outside of the missive and the name Blankenship registered. That lot that drove an old school bus! Back again? Surprised, he handed the envelope to Gert Ealy at the Art Center and waited hopefully for her comment.

Absorbed in a sketch she would show to the afternoon Art class Gert pushed the letter into the pocket of her smock, without any sign of recognition. Purvis was finally forced to leave, his curiosity unsatisfied.

Later, while delivering her daily portion of seed catalogs and gardening journals, he confided this latest news to Marion.

"I tell you I was that surprised when I saw that name. Didn't know whether I should give it direct to Trinity or carry it along to Gert. Her being responsible for Trin all these years."

Marion, encouraged by an hour of almost tepid sunshine, was at work with shovel and spade in the hardened soil at the side of her house. She looked up, smiling at her own efforts against the partial thawing.

"Well, did you ever! Word from the Blankenships! I think you did the right thing. It would surely upset Trinity, hearing from her mother after all this time. Not that Hettie Blankenship was ever much of a mother to any of them. But poor Trinity, as the oldest girl, certainly carried the heaviest load. No, better let Gert handle it. Do you think that crowd has finally decided to recognize their responsibility?"

Purvis laughed, "Kind of a day late and a few dollars short wouldn't you say? It's been all of five years since they pulled out of here."

"Good heavens." Without thinking Marion ran an earthy hand through her hair. "Has it actually been five years since those rascals left here? And not a word from any of them in all this time. After leaving that young girl on her own!"

Marion paused and considered. "Not that she was ever really on her own, so long as Gert and Tom were in town. Which fact the Blankenships were well aware of..."

Shaking her head in disbelief, loosing small particles of dried brush from her bangs in the process, she walked as far as the gate with Purvis.

"Maybe it would be better not to mention this to anyone, just for the time being?"

Purvis nodded in agreement, but Marion crossed her fingers under her thick stack of colorful brochures. Purvis was a good hearted soul, but it wouldn't be easy to keep such an interesting bit of news from spreading, and impossible once he told his wife.

****

Yetta Wiley, wrapped in an aging, rather nondescript coat, settled cheerfully on the seat beside Trinity on the three o'clock bus to Bethany. The three o'clock bus that today is just twenty minutes late. Still dressed in her navy school skirt and white blouse, under a heavy coat sweater, Trinity is keeping her annual appointment with Dr. Monroe, the Dentist. After eleven years of Hettie's simply letting nature take it's course, in the casual Blankenship way, free from medical or dental care, Gert has insisted on regular check-ups. Against Trinity's better judgment.

With her healthy interest in young people, Yetta is rather captivated by the brilliance of Trinity's latest dye job. Red, of a much brighter hue than her own had ever boasted.

Trinity grins in a friendly way. "Do you like my hair Mrs. Wiley? I remember no one was crazy about the golden blond last year, but this is the color your hair used to be isn't it? Everyone said your Henry was so proud of yours. It made all the other women jealous you know."

Overlooking the implied compliment, Yetta smiled inwardly at the phrase, "used to be". Leave it to the young to spell it out loud and clear.

"Oh indeed I do like it. Yes, Henry was always partial to auburn hair of course. But tell me honey, what does Gert think about these changes?"

Trinity gave a carefree shrug. "Oh, she doesn't mind too much. Except that she keeps telling me I'll be bald before I'm old." Trinity giggled. "But Tom thinks it's just another 'phase' so she doesn't make an issue of it."

Then, turning a poetic face toward Yetta, and clutching the somewhat soiled sweater against her heaving chest (Gert had forbidden her to wear it again until it had been washed) a dramatic sigh escapes. She pauses long enough to permit Yetta to savor the full tragedy of her recital. "Tom thinks everything I do is 'just a phase'. Sometimes I think men don't understand a thing about a woman's deep emotional need for beauty and fulfillment." Here she favors Yetta with a truly melodramatic look of resignation, and another gusty sigh.

Yetta controlled a surge of laughter; what movie was that a quote from? She sought another subject. "And where are you off to today dear. Some school function?" Another painful sigh issued forth, and Yetta began to wonder if any subject was without dramatic possibilities to the young.

"No. Gert makes this appointment with Dr. Monroe every year to check my teeth. If she had her way it would be more often. She worries about cavities a lot. Every time she sees me eating something sweet you can see her 'cavity worry look' coming on. She still makes me see Dr. Steele for my physical every year too. Phew! I don't mind that so much any more though. Not since I worked for him last year. It's kind of fun seeing people I used to make appointments for. They're all so friendly." Here she corrected herself. "Well, most of them are".

She laughed. "Mrs. Bernie never has forgiven Dr. for sending her to hospital of course, and he's never forgiven her for leaving without his permission. And Lilly Grigsby starts glaring in his direction before she even goes in his office. She knows he'll start hollering about her weight!"

Yetta, the free spirit, steps warily where other free spirits are concerned; time to change the subject again. She asks innocently, "Are you having a problem dear? Is anything wrong with your health? You look well. Not as husky as some your age but then "it's a lean horse for a long run" as Hery always said."

Trinity's tone brightened. "I like that. Did Henry really say that? I'll remember to tell that to my best friend Gloria when she tells me how much more mature she looks" Then a defensive, almost belligerent statement. "She just has bigger boobs than me." Yetta tried not to wince at the unfamiliar expression and the vacillating humors. Young people!

The bus began to slow and was pulling to a stop, and Yetta was treated to yet another mood swing. "I'm fine Mrs. Wiley. Gert just has this awful guilt thing about being responsible for me. Don't know why she bothers." Her voice wavered slightly, the mascara heavy lashes and red slash of lips receded and her face assumed the vulnerable pucker of a lost infant.

"My own mother wasn't concerned..."

She stiffened, and then swung off the bus. With a frown she began what resembled a reluctant walk to the guillotine.

****

Well, the news of that letter from the Blankenships has set every Village tongue to wagging. Please notice I simply said "the" Blankenships, leaving out all the expletives that are being tossed about by most of us. Even Reverend Marcus hesitates before he answers questions or expresses any opinion. Not that he's likely to discuss their perfidy. Maybe we just want to be sure how far the flock is expected to go in this forgiveness thing after we see what the Shepherd's attitude is.

Purvis, well meaning, but a simple soul, probably intended to keep still about the letter after he talked to Marion. But from what we hear, keeping secrets from Dolly Purvis or old Mrs. P. could be hazardous to his health. Hazel Bernie was privy to the exciting tit-bit only hours after the Post Office closed. Hazel and old Mrs. Purvis have compared notes on Village residents in the past; having been faithful watchers for better than two generations. Fortunately, Purvis does not have x-ray vision, so the exact contents are still unknown. But we will be able to make a reasonable guess I'm sure.

Indignation at the insolence of the Blankenships in even contacting poor Trinity after this stretch of time is warping our judgment. Not that there was much chance of our commendation on any action they might have taken.

The buttercup yellow hair last year caused quite a stir at Liberty High. Had to be dealt with; on a sort of laid back, diplomatic level by Tom, once his eyebrows fell back into place.

Gert hesitated only a second before she touched a springy, glowing curl at Trin's forehead; it remained secure to the scalp; foolishly relieved she hugged the skinny child adult, begging, "Trin, Trin, please, no more changes. A bald headed daughter is not number one on my wish list."

Principal Curry and the School Board searched for any rule that would forbid such a transformation. None was found.

The present brilliant red has Hazel Bernie's own eyebrows raised so high they're almost hidden beneath her hair line. However, Trinity is still Trinity, the pixie girl child abandoned by her parents. And how dare the Blankenships try to get in touch with her after all this time?

Chapter 12
ATTITUDES

I'm afraid the Blankenships still constitute a rather uncomfortable, crumb under the plate experience, in our thinking. It never occurred to any of us that there could be a division in our reaction to the return, only by mail so far, of that wandering tribe. Many of us, when their name is mentioned, assume an expression that says someone has left something ripe unattended. Trinity, with her puppy dog friendliness, has become rather special to most of us. Despite the recurring trauma of trying to recognize her, off hand, in a new hair disguise. She is still Trinity, an exuberant child woman, who gloried in sitting behind the reception desk at Dr. Steele's office for two whole months last year. While the regular receptionist, Patty O'Brian Riley, was busy producing an exceptional, red haired offspring.

That we have not been able to bring our attitudes concerning Trin's wandering parents up to Christian standards is obvious, as we find Mrs. Gillies, mother to Thomasina down in the hollow, beside the counter at the Emporium.

She has seated her considerable weight on a chair Pen dragged from the store room, and is holding court. Loud in her denunciation of anyone opposed to the reunion of Trinity with her *rightful parents.*

"Got no right to ignore a poor mother's suffering you know. Her being held responsible by her Maker for the childs welfare." Her voice rings with a religious fervor. "Just can't never break the true tie between a woman and her daughter." Here she looks about to see if we are appreciating her wonderful mother love wisdom.

With our increasing awareness of her daughter Thomasina's increasing waistline, as she is about to reach her mothers elevated state of motherhood, (in this case with the added status of unwed): and the satisfaction Thomasina reveals as she presents her own welfare check for Pen to cash monthly, we are hard put to retain our composure. Silence is the best that most of us can manage. Lilly Grigsby is forced to leave the area hurriedly before she has a mild stroke.

Hazel Bernie is heard to hiss loudly, “It’s been five years since that trash left town. Never knew it could take that long for a woman to miss a child she loves; if she was in her right mind that is.” At this moment we all find the items we needed, or decide to come back later.

The saga of the wandering Blankenships is winding down. Of the original eleven family members; ten actually exited the Corners in the ailing school bus, there remain only eight. Their exact names may escape us, but their distinct personalities are indelibly printed on the mind of poor Mt. Felson at Edward Graham Elementary. From Ernest, the bright clever one, who formed the habit of helping himself to the other students lunch boxes, to our young ‘Guyus’, Mrs. Blankenship’s hope for the future. Named for the benefactor current at the moment. (Judge Guyus had extricated Mr. Blankenship from a testy I.R.A. official’s grip.)

Old Mrs. Purvis, the postman’s mother kept a list once, with recorded ages. She was wont to bring the list to Hazel Bernie’s attention every nine months with the pious hope that “this was the final tally.” At forty four Nettie Blankenship had given no sign of relinquishing her rights as a female to give life. Sustaining it, once it was given, was evidently not a priority.

Rumor from Minton, where the remainder have taken temporary residence in a government controlled hotel, tells us the two oldest boys broke all family ties as soon as age permitted. The Marine Corp. now boasts two Blankenships. Our only reaction has been gratitude. Perhaps the discipline of the service may undue some of the damage of those early years under their parents languid guidance.

Trinity, after an emotional reunion at the hotel in Minton, has returned to the Corners. To Gert Ealy's very obvious relief and with our wholehearted approval.

****

Reverend Marcus didn't even try to hide his concern when the reunion was instigated; having watched the care and affection which has been lavished on Trinity these past five years by Gert and Tom Ealy. Although childless himself, Marcus has an enormous burden for unloved children.

Poor Tom has experienced all of Trinity's 'rejection' episodes; it took all his tact and wisdom to reassure her of her worth. He has also been the target of her occasional 'hostility' moods, when only one ill advised word could bring on a minor war. Yet he was still grateful when she returned, slammed the front door and threw herself onto the couch for a screaming session of family recrimination.

Tom's curiosity almost overcame him, but under strict orders from Gert, he has asked no questions and offered no advice. If we are lucky Mr. Blankenship's foot will begin to itch again and the whole group will be off to what he envisions as greener pastures. That the green never seems to materialize is not *his* fault, as he affirms to all who will listen. As Miss Bloome from the Bank I am reminded of the English movie, where the results of all human faults and frailties were categorized as "nobody's fault." Are invisible mischief makers rampant throughout the world? Gert and her sister-in-law have given a great deal of thought to the long term affect this filial rejection will have on sweet, rather mixed up, Trinity.

Gert was able to introduce some comfort for the future however. Dr. Angus may be looking for a temporary receptionist yet again. Pretty Patty Riley at the front desk, having produced one robust son so successfully twelve months ago, is now intent on duplication. Trinity could be considered, with the four months working experience last year to her credit.

According to Gert, Trinity's departure would have been felt keenly by her faithful feline sparring partner. At the moment Flinders is making great Balinese type demands as he stands at the front screen door. The solid oak door was left open by mistake by Tom early this morning. "Out, out, out." he howls, with steadily increasing ferocity. Hazel Bernie, his neighbor, is afforded at least one smile each day at his vocal exercises, but his untrained, unrestrained, oriental voice can be a source of irritation to late rising Gert. And because he was de-clawed, before he acquired the Ealy's as royal caretakers, his demands must go unmet.

So Trinity races headlong from the kitchen, the final bite of jelly toast clutched in buttery fingers, bare feet pounding polished hardwood floors. A resounding slam of the offending door settles the Flinders problem for this day.

That it hasn't really helped Gert's day off to a good start should be obvious. But ten minutes later, resigned, Gert creeps down the stairs. Eyes still at half mast she scoops up an indifferent cat body in a forgiving hug and proceeds kitchen ward for coffee and Trinity's latest experiment in cooking. Perhaps burned toast provides carbon needed by the body? She yawns her usual affable "good morning" and faces life among the young and exuberant human world and the old and crotchety animal kingdom.

Chapter 13
GETTING TO KNOW YOU

It's Saturday night, and the buzzing, talk filled dinner hour at the Barn Door is in full swing. Each table filled to capacity with familiar Corner families, or almost as familiar folks who drove over from Bethany. If an unexpected latecomer arrives an extra, unmatched chair can be fetched by Judy from that mysterious store room beyond the kitchen. And a relaxed evening out among their own will be enjoyed by all. While Catagonias, in Bethany, boasts of their *cuisine* the Barn Door just enjoys a widespread reputation for good food, and bonhomie. At prices we can afford, Hazel Bernie is quick to add.

Richard and Geraldine walked to their table, the cheerful one set in a corner window and unconditionally reserved for Richard. An innocent transient diner, seated there in error by Erma, the fill in waitress, could be removed with apologies and soup only half consumed to a less gracious spot; if Richard arrived unannounced. Geraldine wondered idly if being cosseted was habit forming. Wondered, and enjoyed, with only a minimal twinge of guilt. Gregarious Richard has a confident word, or a nod, for most of the diners as they pass. Geraldine smiles a little uncertainly, as she basks in the mixture of curiosity and pleasant acceptance. An almost new feeling of *one-ship* impresses itself warmly on Richard's guiding arm as they reach their table.

Judy and her order pad arrive promptly. Richard knows exactly what he will have, and what Geraldine will order. He hesitates however, and with unexpected solicitude he turns to her for her preference. Geraldine scanned the Barn Door Specials with her usual detachment, brow puckered in polite concentration. If Geraldine has a high priority list, food isn't on it.

He found himself studying her with an unaccustomed warmth. The soft pinks of a filmy summer dress, and he recognizes almost reluctantly, her apparent pleasure in his company, has brought a bloom to Geraldine's now familiar little face. Richard, the willful, the impervious allowed a small, aberrant sensation to escape him; he shook his head and turned, losing the unfamiliar and slightly unnerving incident in the Barn Door's busy chatter.

The service at The Barn Door is as first rate as the menu. Richard is soon enjoying his small steak with baked potato and the essential salad. A smaller portion than in former times, but all that Geraldine allows. In her, Dr. Angus has found a genuine accomplice. The printed diet he recommended for Richard is tacked to her desk at the library as a constant reminder. (Has Richard's state of health become her responsibility?)

Ignoring the salad set before her Geraldine leaned back and let her eyes drift slowly over Richard's face. Noting the strong line of his jaw, the steady, purposeful 'in charge' look. Compelling; was it the confidence she associated with her father? Mental fingers traced the kind lines that were etching over that resolute mask. A mask that was slipping daily? Even a curling tendril of gray hair, escaping from the handsome hair style, suggested heresy.

Transfixed, she watched the now familiar gestures as Richard sipped his wine, touched his mouth with the snowy napkin, and set his glass down carefully. His seemingly remote expression; so aware; yes, she dared to accept the thought, aware of her. Yet so controlled. For a moment his hand lay relaxed and open beside his plate. Geraldine inched forward to slip her own smaller hand into his.

****

Dr. Angus, sitting relaxed at his desk, second story of the Ivy Building, stared moodily out onto Main Street, an opened envelope hanging listlessly from his hand.

A quiet, practically deserted Main Street, at half past six on an early June evening. Long shadows are forming across the pathways as the sun abandons the valley for another day. Elms, vigorous in their finery, are making a dramatic imprint on the old fashioned sidewalks. Like "Oz", Liberty Corners boasts one of the few remaining red brick roads. Abundant burnt sienna clay from our surrounding hills, supplied by an overly generous Maker, paves the four block business Square.

Warm, friendly silence prevails; punctuated now and again by a laugh, or a word, as Albert Hastings moves the metal container of his too early melons off the sidewalk and back into the Emporium for the night. Shipped melons that look good, and even smell ripe, but have still proved themselves to be out of season. Give them another day or two. We are all hungry for the fruits of summer after a long winter.

Birds, their incessant visiting over temporarily are settling sensibly to sleep. Most Cornerites have reached home by now, ready for a good hot meal (with conversation) an hour or so of T.V. (without conversation) and then there are doors to be locked, clocks to be set for wake up time... and so to bed. Following the usual pleasant Liberty Corners eight hour work day.

An eight hour work day for almost everyone, except himself. Angus grinned and shrugged; or Mr. Wilfred of The Morning Sun; at what hour did you put a paper to bed. Albert Hastings of the Emporium Market is still on board, moving slowly but still available. Yetta Wiley probably ran out of yogurt and had to make a last minute emergency trip. Pound right on the glass doors she would, to get his attention; call him from the back room, even when the closed sign was already in place. Come to think of it Liberty Corners never shut down completely, did it?

Now Angus' fingers drummed an impatient tattoo, even while his educated mind was insisting on just the apposite. Take it easy, take it easy, his rational thoughts were urging. It's only a letter so far, just a broad hint that "he is thinking about coming home."

"He," being Dicky Ivy, truant son of one of our founding fathers. The very name, Dicky, can set our collective teeth on edge. We don't have any actual proof, (at least not the proof that Lilly Grigsby accepts) that the bundle of joy carried to Liberty Corners one stormy night about twenty four years ago, and presented to Richard as his natural son, was genuine. By a young woman we had never seen before... or since!

Richard O. Ivey, giver of bounties to worthy causes, and strong advocate of our almost militant independence. He it is who gave us the video series "Seeing America First" now showing at the library monthly, to the delight of out super patriots; and several new Computers for Liberty High when the School District cried the poor mouth.

Following the death of Richard's wife, Mary Beth, days and nights have been lonely, even for the one we call our 'lone ranger.' Now Richard has finally achieved a pleasant relationship with Miss Geraldine. A relationship that could be permanent... barring any disruptions...

Richard may bully us without mercy at Village Meetings, when we have opposing views, which is often, but we are convinced that a heart of gold must lurk under that sometimes forbidding exterior.

Chapter 14

THAT CAT!

Eight A.M. Saturday morning. Tom Ealy began to stir, if only a little against his will. No clients, no appointments, Real Estate in the doldrums in this area, at the moment. Maybe he should get some of those flower beds cleared out; the rose border Gert had mentioned so sweetly only three times in the last month? Richard Ivy's landscape job last fall has caused all the other Cornerites to notice how shabby their own gardens were beginning to look. Property pride and competition is friendly and low key with us, but rampant. He wrinkled his nose, and tried to sink back into the warm crevice of blankets.

Gert's drowsy attention caught the slight movement; she turned to move a restraining arm across his chest, pinning him with languid affection. "Don't even think about taking off on your own this morning," she threatened sleepily, "You promised to help me get the 'DO' more organized, remember." Tom's resistance is minimal as he relaxes beneath the familiar pressure.

"We don't have to start on that yet, do we? It's still months away."

His half hearted complaint falls on deaf ears, so he shifts to a more comfortable position; his eyes close, convinced that wily weeds will still be creeping in to displace the legal owners of the rose beds next week, so why sweat it.

An hour later, and not yet thoroughly awake, Tom pushed into position at the kitchen table, rubbed a crumpled pajama sleeve across his eyes, and then stared, transfixed. A hundle of beige and brown fur exploded past his upraised arm and disappeared under the hanging folds of the tablecloth; to be followed quickly by a determined girl child body clad in shorts and a 'T' shirt. He listened to a moment of desperate scuffling; cat claws punished shiny linoleum; girl knees and elbows knocked against chair legs, and then: "Ha... gotcha!."

Trinity has grasped Flinders in a strangle hold, a hold which he usually loves. Flinders let out a murderous oriental curse, and Tom lifted an edge of the tablecloth to peer anxiously.

"Trin, what in the world..."

Flinders was making wide passes with his claw-less front paws, at Trinity's face, even as his jaws grasped the remains of what looked to be a small, rather dead, kitchen mouse. Trinity gave one quick grin upward.

"Oh it's okay Tom. I'm just trying to get the rest of this away from him before he can swallow it... Ouch... Flinders, hold still you devil cat... Oh, now you've done it!"

With a final wrench she pulled a tattered remnant from his grasp and released him. Flinders emerged, tail erect, and with a disdainful toss of his head; a triumphant actor completing a successful scene.

Trinity crawled into view and Tom dropped the edge of the cloth he had been clutching. Refusing to consider what remained in her hands he shuddered and leaned back against his chair as Trinity headed for the kitchen sink.

"Not in the disposal, not in the disposal," he almost begged.

Trinity allowed herself one withering shrug in Tom's direction as she headed for the alley trash container. "Adults! Especially men!"

Tom pushed lukewarm coffee aside to join the already unwelcome burnt toast.

****

A sleepy Gert has joined the breakfast group. Tom surveys the thoroughly inscrutable face of the cat body that has now draped itself insolently over the arm of his chair, and offers a tentative suggestion...

"Don't you think it's about time this old war lord had some competition for attention around this house; another cat maybe, a kitten. Or... what about a dog? It would have to be one old enough..."

"And crafty enough", Gert suggested.

"Yes," Tom agreed "one with plenty of smarts, to protect its rights against the reigning monarch. But still young enough to offer some companionship?"

Tom looked first at Gert, and then at Trin for confirmation of his rather brilliant proposal. Gert started to grin but Trin laughed out loud.

"You've got to be kidding. A kitten! Old Flin wouldn't put up with a kittens nonsense for five minutes. And... can you see a dog putting up with Flin's nonsense?" Doubled with laughter Trin almost fell from her chair as she considered Flinders sharing friendship or companionship with any size dog.

"It would probably take a Rotweiler to cope with Flinders disposition," Gert admitted," a female maybe, suffering from mid life depression."

Trin and Gert shook their heads in disbelief as Tom continued thoughtfully "I think he might be lonesome... I really do. We're gone most of the time, and Trin, well, after all, she's one of the human or problem species. Anyway I think it's worth thinking about."

He refilled his coffee cup, and abandoned the table, and the problem.

****

A peaceful breakfast interlude was shattered following what an aggrieved Tom swore was an innocent inquiry: "What did they decide about Mr. Felson's plan to feature his first graders in the 'DO' this year?" That was all he had asked.

Unfortunately it was too early in the morning, and too early in the year for decisions concerning the 'DO', and besides, poor Gert had had an early morning telephone call from Lilly Grigsby, (an ear shattering call shared almost equally between the outraged barking of Darling Mauvaleen and the outraged queries of her devoted owner). She had replaced the receiver, totally unenlightened, and with a strange tendency to snap at everybody she met.

"I need time to think! I need time to think. I'm getting questions on all sides about the changes we're planning this year, and I don't have any concrete answers from Guyus and Richard yet." Pushing away from the breakfast table after this impassioned plea, which fell an deaf ears, she snatched the final crust of her toast in a paper napkin and headed down the hall.

Gert stepped into her broom closet office, rehung the Don't Disturb sign in its place and closed the door to her spiritual cell. The door, and the hand printed sign, that guaranteed privacy and sanctity against a super active teenaged female and a stealthy, feline despot.

Sun, rich and warm poured in the south window; Hazel Bernie's tall elms formed a solemn fringe of velvet shade at the property line. Gert's whole body relaxed; she sank into the familiar, comfortably worn chair that accommodated every curve of her body; A 'Peace that passeth understanding' moment reined.

Then a minute sound invaded, and her eye found a supine, deliciously innocent, cat figure stretched in vulnerable repose beneath her desk. Beige and golden fur almost lost against the pale earth tone rug. The rectangle of faded wool that had become another of his personal 'homes away from home.' A guileless head propped against an outstretched paw, eyes closed in sweet surrender. Furry sides raised and lowered gently; small scruffy cat sounds floated upwards.

"Good Lord," Gert shook her head in disbelief," Flinders has developed a snore!"

Suddenly, the warning sign not withstanding, the door behind her burst open. Trinity stopped just short of knocking Gert from her chair. An embarrassed laugh and an apology followed.

"Sorry Gert. Flinders got away from me and I can't find the pesky bugger anywhere."

It took just a glance past Gert, and Trinity gave a war whoop. A sound that brought an immediate reaction from the pesky bugger. A wild struggle broke out with girl recriminations and cat denials, and only ended when Flinders, evading clutching hands, made a dignified exit. He hesitated only long enough to offer a small compensatory nip at Trinity's heel.

Chapter 15

'FAMOUS BY MISTAKE' JELLY

Grinning, Marion pushed the half empty jam jar into Gert's outstretched hand. Gert's eyebrows raised slightly. "We're running short of preserves at Lozier's diner? Charlie must have been entertaining all his hungry friends again."

"Don't be crabby, girl. I'm sharing the very last tablespoons of my 'Famous by Mistake' concord jelly. My old vine produced only enough grapes for six glasses, and you are enjoying the final spoon fulls in the final glass. Last year's bounty has disappeared."

She gave a resigned sigh. "I should have waited till I had more time to do jelly properly, but I was in a rush, as usual. But after the first taste of that jelly I realized that I had outclassed myself. I didn't have a clue why it was so much better. Then I recalled how I had washed the grapes thoroughly, shed all the extra moisture and popped them, almost dry, into my mother's old copper kettle on low heat. Meaning to get back immediately to add the necessary water as usual. Only you know Charlie. He needed my attention at that moment. And the grapes prepared themselves. For the grandest juice I ever had. A minimum of sugar produced what Charlie insists on calling my 'Famous by Mistake' recipe."

Gert applied a generous dab of Concord jelly to an already buttered roll and allowed herself one bite, then she grinned. "Well, by mistake or not, it's the best grape jelly I've ever tasted. And you know I consider myself a grape jelly expert."...

A final delicious taste... Almost automatically her fingers stretched toward the remaining rolls. She drew back, tucked her hands beneath the napkin in her lap and shook her head at Marion's rather obvious urging, "No, no, no. Dr. Angus is going to put me on his 'Most Difficult to Cope With' patient list before my fortieth birthday thanks to your cooking genius. Along with

Richard and Hazel." Her tone changed, "Now what do you mean disappeared? Has Corners become a victim of the world's petty thievery syndrome? Or have you, as usual, given away all the company's profits?"

Marion, still flushed with pride at the compliment, smiled self consciously.

"Well, I was kind of saving the last jar for myself. Probably being selfish and self centered Mama might have said, but Charlie opened it by mistake."

"He really did, open by mistake, I mean." she insisted.." It seems the boy he considers his older friend, Barry Thornton, had had an exciting dining experience and he shared it with all of his buddies," Marion began to explain.

"It required crackers, and soft cheese and jelly. Well, there were crackers in my cupboard, even a small jar of cheese, but only one glass of jelly left on the shelf.

I guess Barry had run out of resources one afternoon, and decided to visit with his next door neighhor, Miss Campbell from the College. He feels he's always welcome, and of course he is, but having so little real contact with children, I suspect the poor soul was just trying to think of some way to entertain him So, knowing that eight year olds (Barry stretches the truth a little when he claims nine already) are hollow, clear to their shoe tops, she suggested they have a genuine *English Tea.* An Americanized version of course, she explained, since she did not have any cucumbers for sandwiches. Which must have been a real confusion to Barry. I'm sure he never encountered a cucumber in any state except as a pickle on his hamburger.

Barry was enchanted when he discovered the tea included mounds of open faced sandwiches, cheese spread liberally on saltine crackers by Miss Campbell, leaving a center hole. That he was actually pressed into service, by Miss Campbell herself, to fill all the holes, too generously I imagine, with his own selection of jams, was the crowning touch to a memorable afternoon...Barry's tea was actually only milk from Grant's dairy served in a lovely china cup with boiling water and a sugar lump added. Splendor! Miss Campbell told me he held the cup very carefully, his little finger extended, like he saw in a movie once, and made only small sucking sounds, to capture the last delicious drops. The 'Party' was such a memorable success that Charlie has been demanding a replay ever since."

Marion hesitated slightly, and grinned, "I'm sure Miss Campbell knew her mother would find the whole idea agreeable too." As one of the United Methodist 'Fruit Cake Ladies' Mrs. Zona Campbell has made us aware that appetites do not necessarily abate in late years. Especially when all molars are intact and prodigious amounts of pecans are available.

"Anything different, and what he considers adult, gets Barry's attention. Especially when there is food involved."

Chapter 16

ANOTHER REUNION & A PROBLEM

This may be recorded in our Liberty Corners annals as the year of reunions. First there was the Blankenship's temporary return. Fortunately they only stayed long enough to; #l Raise the blood pressure level of both Hazel Bernie and Mrs. Purvis to a dangerous level and #2 Obtain a free health examination provided by Dr. Angus. Hettie B. had been complaining of low back pain and was concerned that she was once again "with child" A quaint expression she has adopted against our mundane 'pregnant'.

And now Loretta Crum is back on the scene. As trim and lacquered as before, she simply walked into the Emporium with a long list of needs. Pen said she almost lost her lower plate when she looked up and saw her. She admitted Hazel Bernie's expression 'brassy hussy' did come to mind, but she kept her cool and accepted a rather large packet of cash to cover a few staples, and an incredible amount of cleaning supplies. Loretta offered a humorous grin to Pen as she lifted three cans of cleansing powder, a gallon size bottle of Deep Clean and two spray cans of spot remover. "You can see Crum didn't wear himself out with housework while I was gone" she laughed. "Never was much for taking care of his own place, too busy doing for the rest of you. Well, I'll get him straightened out, pronto, believe me." Pen says it did occur to her to wonder who needed the straightening out most but she was still too shocked to answer. Just rang up the sale and helped Loretta load her car.

Most of us don't know exactly how to handle it. With Crum being such a general favorite, and indispensable in our daily battles. Drain pipes that insist on getting clogged, and furnaces that develop kinky problems at the wrong time of the year. At the time of her unannounced, and unexplained leave taking, our sympathies were naturally geared to the forsaken husband.

Although Hazel Bernie had her own opinion about how great a genuine loss he had suffered. But how we hate mysteries, especialy those that occur right under our noses. Even though we have real talent in coming to conclusions that satisfy us. Even totally inaccurate conclusions.

****

Gert Ealy opened Marion's kitchen door and then hesitated. No cheery welcome, no response to her arrival at all! Complete silence, in Marion's house? She stepped to the dining room door and stopped.

Completely unaware, Marion rubbed a polishing cloth pensively across the scarred table top in her west window. Her usual energetic movements were slowed to a disconsolate push and pull, even as her lips moved. "Have to move this table," she muttered," getting too much sun... Something else I haven't taken proper care of, I guess."...

A stubby finger tenderly eased the double picture of Charlie; before his first birthday, in the fragile, embroidered baby dress, that had rather discomforted his modem mother; and again at age two in what his mother called a 'jump suit' more to her liking. Marion eased the frame closer to the center. A strong breeze could knock it over and shatter the glass. She murmured a fervent "God forbid'"and gave a final pat.

Gert finally cleared her throat, rather self consciously.

Marion turned, surprised. "For goodness sake, I didn't even hear you come in. Senility setting in, or already full blown maybe?"

Gert hesitated, noted the pensive face and rather solemn greeting. "Hi Mar. What's going on? I thought you were coming down to the studio this afternoon to see my latest landscape."

"I meant to. Started out in that direction... But then I had some fresh biscuits left over from breakfast that I knew Hazel Bernie would enjoy. She's partial to the cheese ones you know."

"Who isn't? And of course you thought you could just stop by for a minute". Gert laughed. "There is no such thing as a one minute call on Hazel Bernie. Charlie could have told you that. He spends hours with her and her 'spy glass'."

Marion grimaced slightly. "I know, she reminded me of the fact. I felt I should apologize. Maybe I'm being neglectful, and he's a bother."

"For heaven's sake, Mar!. Charlie makes Hazel's day. In his idle chattering he probably gives her more inside news about all of us than she could get at the Emporium. She doesn't go to Church often enough to keep current. Besides, just think of the pressure his visits take off poor Lila Mae."

Marion nodded, but still pursued a troubling thought. "Gert, you must know more about children than I do. All I know is poor little Charlie. And his friends, of course."

"Which is five or six more than I have any contact with," Gert admitted, "but what's bothering you'?"

Marion straightened her back and challenged Gert.

"Gert do you think Charlie is developing an inferiority complex?"

Gert stared in unbelief, and then burst out laughing.

"Is Charlie doing what...?"

Marion, obviously concerned, repeated. "Developing an inferiority complex. Hazel thinks he may be. She insists with no father figure, or what she calls 'male model influence' he is bound to be, well, she called it 'psychologically warped'. It's a term they use on that T.V. program she watches. Whatever it is, she's convinced he's doomed, and I'm responsible."

Here she sank into her chair, her head in her hands." I came home after one hour, and seriously considered placing Charlie up for adoption before I 'warp' him any further."

Pooh-poohing the whole subject and aghast at poor Marion's state of mind Gert rescued her purse and portfolio from the couch where she had tossed them in her agitation, and was actually set to confront Flinders friend Hazel, consequences be damned, when the kitchen door burst open.

One look brought Marion to her feet in alarm. "Charlie, Charlie, what have you done?"

Charlie, with a very ripped shirt, and a lip that was rapidly increasing in size and changing in color, reached for Marion's outstretched hands.

"It's okay Gram, honest it's okay." he pleaded bravely. "I'm okay, really... You should see Guyus Gillies. He looks worse than me..."

Little comforted, Marion, with one glance at Gert, and without waiting for any explanation, grasped Charlie's shoulder with a firm hand and started for the bathroom and sanitary measures.

Still inflated with his imaginal victory Charlie shouted to Gert as he was led down the passage, "Aunt Gert, Crum made us stop fighting but he says I have such a good left hook I'll probably grow up to be a prize fighter... What is a 'left hook', Aunt Gert?"

Chapter 17
CONCERNS

Even as Noel watched 'Judge' Carpentar disappeared momentarily; a smiling and benign Guyus Carpentar leaned back in his chair, eyes half closed, and considered Cordelia. Calm and remote Cordelia Wiley, the librarian, that Beulah's enthusiastic sanguine son Noel was determined to marry. A lovely girl, heavy chestnut hair framed a cautiously friendly face, an almost timid smile was vying with obvious concern. Establishing, for the first time, what must be a lifetime relationship with a *possible-impossible* father-in-law?

Village born actually, a fringe member of Pastor Severns congregation, he understood. With an attractive, rather outspoken Jewish mother. His mind touched on the often suspect village reports; Jewish, now Christian Scientist, head of a group in Bethany calling themselves 'Positive Thinkers.' He gave a grunt; nothing wrong with that.

Cordelia, relaxed as much as possible, seated next to his son on Beulah's colorful couch in his own quiet living room. Sitting next to, but not crowded against, he noticed. A small affirming note escaped him. He looked at the two of them but his attention lingered on the girl. As pretty a girl as Beulah herself had been; but so quiet, calm; such a contrast to Noel's intense, enthusiastic approach to life. He was just like his mother; was this a repetition of his own marriage? He settled back in his chair. Yes, Beulah would have been content with Noel's choice.

"So now, what are your plans...?" His tone was affable, almost affectionate. Its very sensitivity caught Noel off guard. The question was meant for Cordelia. That his own intentions were clear, he knew. He glanced uncertainly at Cordelia and then at Guyus. An embarrassed grin spread over his face. "Well now Dad, Cordy hasn't exactly..."

As she still hesitated Guyus leaned forward to place a hand rather cautiously on her arm "Have you decided on a definite date my dear?" Cordelia, not quite prepared for such a direct approach hesitated. Guyus cleared his throat." You are definitely planning on marriage?" Familiarity with todays world rankled; his tone assumed the authority of a Court order; the sound ruled out any alternative.

Noel drew an unresisting Cordelia closer.

"Of course we're going to be married. As soon as 'Cordy' (his voice lingered over the beloved name) when Cordy decides on a day."

His new found confidence spread a wonderful warmth over what had promised to be a chilly meeting. Cordelia found herself wanting to please him.

"We have a lifetime ahead of us," she offered almost apologetically, "an unwise decision now... I just need," unconsciously she stressed the last word," to be very sure that I'm making the right decision. Not just for me, but for all of you, as well"

Here she turned abruptly toward Guyus. "Judge Carpentar, you know my mother, Hattie?"

Guyus nodded and waited. A questioning frown creased his forehead.

"So you know I'm Jewish. At least half of me is. This isn't going to bother you, or stand in the way ___ of a genuine family relationship ______?"

At his silence she argued on. "It may concern some in the Village," she emphasized," and this is your home turf." She paused, her deepest concern released.

Clutching Noel's hand she hoped she was making sense. Practical, reasonable and logical sense, which the Judge would respect. After all, she was addressing Noel's father, a man she could he related to for the rest of their lives. The grandfather of her children! A sobering thought.

Guyus, who had spent fifty years listening to miscreants in what he heard termed 'the Liars Court' sat for a full minute studying an earnest young face before him. Deeply touched, as Cordelia said, “Are you sure you would welcome a Jewish daughter-in-law?”

Eyes misting, he laid his hand gently on hers.

“Cordelia, my dear, I only wish Beulah had lived to see the happiness you have brought to Noel, and now to me.” Relieved by her explanation of any delay, Guyus shook his head and offered a tremulous smile.

“If being a Jew, or should I say Jewess, is your only problem... Pastor Marcus has a church full of what he terms ‘born again Seeds of Abraham’, including me and my household. Can you get more Hebrew than that?”

Chapter 18

CHILDREN

Marion smiled at Lila Mae Bernie, relaxed comfortably in Marion's own particular recliner this late summer afternoon; a tall glass of iced tea in hand. None of the jumbo oat meal cookies, thank you. Paper thin Lila Mae avoids sweets.

Marion, towels in hand, wrestled with three squirming, dripping, giggling boys, just retrieved from the 'Super Cyclone' back yard fountain and pool. Purchased one week ago by Marion at a greatly reduced price due to the fast approaching fall season, and after only minor financial calculations; (would Judge Guyus consider this as a necessary expenditure? Especially if installed free of charge by Tom Ealy and Arthur Grigsby?) With a little more than supervisory help from Crum, since neither Arthur's back nor Tom's increasing girth could manage the necessary digging of trenches for laying pipe.

The fountain has been an outstanding success. Drawing in friends of Charlie's, many from down in the Hollow of whom poor Marion was not aware. Ivy's boisterous dog Dracula, loosed by mistake by a village child, has been a super active and violently vocal unwelcome addition to the party.

Straining to be heard over the the increasing bedlam Marion attempted to explain her problem. Even as she ushered half dried bodies toward the table for snack time.

"Sorry for the mess," she apologizes, "The pool in some ways, is a minor catastrophe, but getting the children to the Y.M.C.A. in Bethany to swim every day or so, was a catastrophe of major proportions, believe me!"

Her voice rose as her hands pressed the rough towel again and again over Charlie's wet bobbing head.

"Hold still honey, hold still just one more minute." With an indulgent laugh she urges patience on the perpetual motion object she is trying to administer to.

"It's dry Gram, it's dry," Charlie insists almost frantically, his eyes fixed on the diminishing stack of cookies. Marion released her hold, and shook her head; another chair scraped into place at the big comfortable table.

Lila Mae held her breath as a pitcher of Grant's whole cream milk, fresh from the refrigerator, began to pass from hand to outstretched hand... Hopefully without spilling?

Marion continued. "Just driving down town turned out to be a parade. First there was me, with my car full. Charlie, and Legs, and Barry Thornton. Then Clemmy Lukes with her car packed. She carried all three little girls, and Ben, when he didn't have a soccer game going or practice at First Christian."

She paused. "As Choir director, Alma Grant is already making big plans for our Hospitality Week, which you know." Lila Mae, First Christians main stay nodded.

"And if the Gillies children let us know in time, Gert Ealy would slip away from the Art Class to carry them. She would have included Trinity in the outing too, of course, but poor Trinity is suffering the pangs of near adulthood, feels herself too far above the antics of these young ones.

Gert said the one time Trin deigned to accompany them, she swam clear at the other end of the pool, and disassociated herself from the lot, until it was time to drive home. Would have avoided them even then if she had any other transportation!"

Lila Mae accustomed to children walking in a subdued fashion in the House of God, wondered how Marion maintained her wonderful cheerful aplomb amidst the savage throng?

****

Ben Lukes has become the proud owner of a rather strange looking dog. At least he *hopes* to become the owner. But Aunt Clemmy is still praying against that hope; perhaps Gramps will veto the whole project?

A stray, of massive proportions, with what appears to be two left front legs that operate at their own discretion; collarless, it followed Ben from the Family Market in Bethany, and uninvited, leaped into the back seat of Clemmy's Buick as the door was opened. And was deaf to all commands to leave.

Clemmy, the dangerous daisy hat partly obscuring her view, stood in the parking lot undecided. Her armload of packages were not only getting very heavy, but beginning to veer right and left. Afraid to get too close, she could only plead and beseech the beast to step out onto the parking lot. Barking joyously from the back seat, he settled comfortably. A dog used to traveling?

Emmy, Poppy, and Kursty fascinated, and unwilling to climb aboard until the matter is settled, screamed admonitions to Auntie "Don't hurt the poor thing" and offered promises of safe harbor to this exciting new recruit to Clemmy's household.

Clemmy had no intention of moving near enough to 'hurt' the poor thing, but the great unwashed body was filling the back seat and, in fact, bulging forward against the drivers seat in an alarming way. Recriminations broke out, of course, with Auntie accusing Ben of enticing the beast to follow in some way.

"You're just too friendly, you encouraged him. Now what in the world are we going to do with him?" By this time Clem was near tears.

"Not so Auntie, I didn't speak to him," Ben protested. "Didn't know his name, how could I speak to him."

Now however Ben laid a tentative hand on the shaggy head with a murmured "Poor old man." The gesture was received enthusiastically with a very moist tongue, and the lumpy body lodged itself more securely in it's new space. Fearing Clem would dissolve in her woe Ben offered a timid solution.

"Tell you what Auntie, Why don't we just let him ride on home with us and let Gramps get him out. Gramps can handle any animal." Since no other answer offered itself, Ben crawled in the opposite door of the back seat, was welcomed with lordly affection by the new tenant and the ride back to Liberty Corners began. Almost without incident.

Chapter 19

MISS BLOOME-NEE NELLIE BLODGETT

After thirty wonderful years of daily association with some really nice folks in an enduring, turn of the century Village, nothing should surprise me, I guess. But it is atrange, isn't it, how we notice advanced age in others with such a shock, while our own 'withering on the vine' goes almost unnoticed? I was shopping in Bethany yesterday and was greeted, in a shrill commanding voice, just as I was leaving National Dry Goods; by an ancient lady, in an equally ancient green hat.

"Nellie, Nellie Blodgett," she kept calling, in a distinctly irritated way. Having been 'Miss Bloome from the Bank' for so many years my true identity didn't register. I simply continued walking toward my car parked at the curb. Only to have my elbow caught by steel reinforced fingers, as a raspy voice demanded "You are Fannie Blodgett's daughter, I know you are," she accused. "You couldn't fool me with that nose. I'd know that nose anywhere."

By now I am pulled to a stand still as we block shoppers on the sidewalk, and she peers intently over her steel framed spectacles.

"Yes indeed, I'd know that nose anywhere" she insists. "She was my closest friend you know, next door neighbors in Grafton."

I take a second look. My poor mother has been gone some fifteen years. What age must this person be? The pulsing throng having no affect, I urged her toward an empty spot near the National's front window. Hoping that no one had a sudden urgency to look at winter blankets, now on sale and piled in colorful profusion; or distinct noses.

I found myself apologizing. For not knowing my maiden name when it is called out on a public street, or for not recognizing my mother's neighbor of some fifty years past, I don't know which. For the reference to 'the nose' I feel an apology is due me, but assume that none will be forthcoming, and insisting might prolong this assault.

"I'm afraid I don't recall your name dear. Didn't even remember my own name." Is it possible to forget your maiden name, or is this a sure sign of altsheimers?" I held out my hand.

"Has it been many years since we met?"

She finally offered some reluctant fingers wrapped in worn black gloves which I accepted warily, having already experienced their pressure on my elbow. A wintry smile was offered and I tried to return with a little warmth.

Perhaps her memory is as faulty as mine; she could not recall the date that I had made my final journey back. Which was a blessing really, since the trip had not been a happy event and I had no desire to relive it again with her. Burying my little mother in Trinity Church cemetery in the lot next to where my father lay at peace had closed the door on the past. Me and my distinct 'nose' had never looked back.

****

Advancing age and 'the nose' not withstanding I was one of the first invited to view the restoration of the Mansion. The Beazleys were able to complete their work, despite delivery problems, almost on time. Not quite complete yet. All new appliances ordered from National Dry Goods in Bethany have not arrived.

Having stopped off at Marion Lozier's for fresh ginger root, just as Richard made his afternoon survey of the project, he invited, well, almost urged Marion and me in to view a little of what the whole village had been waiting to see. That he actually wanted our opinion was interesting. We were as anxious to see as Richard was to exhibit.

Strange, Richard has always tended to be extremely private, actually reproved poor MaryBeth for disclosing any of their personal life. Even Marion Lozier, from her house right next door, did not cross that line. The fact that Charlie was the innocent witness to a few irate outbursts at MaryBeth's candid friendliness Marion never repeated. And now he is seriously involved with someone just as reserved as he used to be. And wants to show the wonderful changes that he obviously intends for her. All under her directions, we are sure.

While the original trips to the library may have been for research on his business interests, it wasn't long after the first *date* (the teenage volunteers incredulous definition of dinner or a drive in Richard's, *fresh from Wilbanks Car Wash,* Cadillac) before the same little vipers were betting on exciting possibilities as they re-shelved endless decorating books. Copious notes on scraps of Geraldine's personal note paper, with page numbers, and added cryptic messages were retrieved from the waste basket. The renewing of the entire kitchen area captures our attention. Are we witnessing a metamorphosis from timid bookworm to competent housewife?

Though the remodeling and the obvious personal involvement of Geraldine in Richard's future, if he has his way, is clear; no definite wedding day has been announced. Richard being Richard, we would still hesitate to ask him. And Geraldine's sweet deference to his leading keeps us from overstepping his boundaries. Now however, the fact that she is planning an unexpected short trip to her sister's in California, for no apparent reason, has a few eyebrows raised.

That she has been hesitant about admitting to a romantic involvement this late in her life we understand. And that she would want her sister's approval for any decision she might make. But Richard's sudden decision to accompany her to her sister's in California is grist for any ones mill, right?

We are all anxious that nothing stand in the way of what appears to us to be a happy solution for two lonely people. As Richard's personal physician, Dr. Angus couldn't be more pleased. Loneliness can produce too many side issues that he doesn't feel qualified to deal with. He is convinced that marriage to a mature, no nonsense woman. (sweetly submissive

Geraldine took issue with Dicky's demands by mail once before, remember) may settle the errant son problem finally. Besides the man is obviously in love.

Chapter 20
FAMILIAR DAILYS

Little Main, as the street that continues beyond the Square is referred to, has become one long solo of a cutting, shearing, trimming melody every Monday, and again on alternate Fridays. Crum has taken over the gardening chores of all of us who live in that area. Handymen are hard to find, even in villages, and we are so grateful that he has consented to cover our needs while Manuel is gone.

Hopefully to be gone only temporarily. We have become quite dependent on Manuel's expertise when cantankerous weather patterns have plagued us. That the sudden return to Mexico was occasioned by family problems we were told; as he loaded an excited Pedro into the waiting Chevvie, wiry arms clutching a large hamper provided by the United Methodists and numerous small possessions. Money matters, we are sure. Manuel has been saving his monthly wages from Ebert, as well as extra monies provided by others, in a savings account at Interstate Bank. Upon his arrival in the Village Miss Bloome had taken him and his finances wisely in hand. From his first pay day. While the small possessions are important to Pedro, the hamper is indispensable. Meat sandwiches of goodly proportions, carefully wrapped in plastic wrap, plus a generous sack of Marion's oatmeal cookies, *this time with chocolate chips,* as well as several cans of orange soda: the only soft drink Marion permits in Charlie's diet. The hamper weighs heavy, but cannot safely be trusted to the back of the truck, so Pedro's seat must he adjusted to fit an even smaller person. It rests safely against his legs, comfortably within reach of his hands. Like a gas tank registering empty, his tummy was already emitting minor protests as the truck took off.

So Miss Bloome as well as others are relying on already overworked Crum. While her gardening services will demand only ordinary cutting and edging, Crum will also be in charge of seeing after the birds needs. Birds have always been a big issue with Miss Bloome; ornery blue jays who fight and argue endlessly, graceful, sedate morning doves who walk about like ecclesiastics with a definite preference for sunflower seeds. As well as the humble, but odiously persistent sparrows.

That her fruit trees are responsible for her biggest problem; dung encrusted bannisters, dung encrusted cushions on chairs and her beloved porch swing, as well as instant, jagged holes in every available pear or apple as the first shadow of ripening occurs, she is aware. But as the fruit season wanes she finds guilt taking over, she refills the canister with the *Family Market's Special Domesticate Bird Seed,* at two dollars for a five pound bag, and sets the fountain into action that the creatures may drink and eat and bathe in an orderly fashion. Between Marion and Miss Bloome birds do well in Liberty Corners…

****

Crum pulled his truck, now clean and surprisingly orderly with Loretta back in charge, into the driveway beside the library building. The Richard Ivy wing was due for a thorough fall cleaning and perhaps some minor repairs before its use again this year during the 'Do.' The puppet show last year in the little improvised theater had been a great success. Featuring sometimes unorthodox adventures of 'Pooh Bear' it had brought enthusiastic children for three days running. From outlying communities as well as our own. An idea created by Cordelia under the direction of Miss Campbell from the college. That it had opened up dramatic possibilities to Guyus Gillies, as well as his best friends was evident for weeks following. Their theatrical ambitious were cut short by poor Mr. Felson. At least while under his jurisdiction.

Crum drew the key from his pocket and inserted it into the still almost new, brass lock. A key entrusted to him since the grand opening of the controversial wing. He smiled to himself.

What would the new arrangements be, with both Geraldine and Cordelia about to take on new identities? Would the library continue to operate under the competent direction of Geraldine Ivy? He couldn't quite accept the idea of Richard Ivy playing second fiddle to a job. Not hardly! And would Noel want to share his wife's time with all the avid readers in the Village? A perplexed Crum pulled the sweeper from the utility room and began his clean up.

****

Guyus Carpenter, with even an hour of free time on his hands, is a danger to all of us. So, after several false starts, he has reorganized the AWG'S, our adult walking group. The list already includes Mr. Wilfred of 'The Sun', whose arthritis has been kicking up; Ebert Grant from Old Farm; and Arthur Grigsby, whose over riding belly, pressed against the table at the last meeting, had been noted. The reprehensibles are finding reasons to avoid that early morning exercise agony. Some excuses offered so lame you wouldn't believe!

Surprise hovered behind a rather dour greeting when Lila Mae Bernie stopped by the Judge's house early one morning to announce she intended to be included in the program. Pleased, yet puzzled, he welcomed her with wary warmth; not an ounce of flesh to spare, not exactly young, but younger than the others involved, maybe she just needed a break from Hazel? They shared a cup of Hulda's less than perfect cocoa, and Guyus listened to a recital of Marcus' latest financial concerns. Listened, and made a note for his wallet.

That Tom Ealy has actually agreed to join was noteworthy. But perhaps Tom's initial enthusiasm had overstated the joys of early morning jogging in his discussion at the breakfast table? For, while Guyus languished at Pen's cash register at the Emporium early one morning Trinity Blankenship touched his arm and informed him that she was joining his group, convinced it was time she too 'got in shape.' He hardly recognized the red headed young thing addressing him politely as Judge Carpenter; and the less than a hundred pounds of girl in a torn T shirt and shorts appeared to be in optimum condition... But a recruiting Sergeant doesn't argue with possibilities. If he counted himself, the seven was now complete.

Chapter 21
CONVERSATIONS

"You may be ashamed to have me at your door," Amy Grant apologized as Marion closed the inner door against late summers determined assault. It's early Tuesday morning and Amy Grant, trailing a nondescript housecoat, has just dropped into the comfortable rocking chair in Marion Lozier's still cool kitchen. Ostensibly to take possession of as many of Marion's special fresh herbs as Marion can spare. Literally dropped, she would be the first to admit, as the heat that struck her as she exited her air conditioned truck was overpowering.

Marion, after a welcoming but brief, hot weather hug, looked down at the somewhat worse for wear garment that drooped from her own shoulders and made a derisive face.

"I'm a mess too" she moaned. "I wake up around five, rested and full of good intentions. The house is still cool, and Charlie isn't up yet. He's been sleeping later these hot days, thank heavens. And I know how many things I didn't get finished yesterday." She paused as she poured fresh water into the waiting coffee pot. "So I just pull this poor old float on over my gown, intending to dress properly after my coffee."

She grinned at Amy. "And yes, it's the same float I bought on sale for fifteen dollars when National Dry Goods had their close out, five and a half years ago, remember?."

Amy nodded. "I know just what you mean. I jump out of bed set to move a few mountains, or at least shift a few of our foothills... I only have to step outside after the sun takes over though, and I can feel Marcus' enemy, that old 'spirit of procrastination' taking control." The mention of Marcus' special foes brings on a smile. The ones that were rife in the congregation?

"Ebert threatened to burn my favorite old rose robe last week if he had to look at it one more time. Imagine, and I've only had it ten years.! When August rolls around the name of the game seems to be *Comfort.* And here I am at half past eight, supposed to be on my way to pick up Cordelia Wiley. Soon to be Cordelia Carpentar, right? And the Circle meets at nine."

"Cordelia has always been active in that group, hasn't she? Especially if there were kids involved? Yetta is the same way, only she tends to enjoy teen agers more. I hope Cordelia will have some children of her own, don't you? Neal should make a great father. And Yetta would love being a grandmother."

"An energetic, positive thinking grandmother, mind!" Amy insisted. "No negative old lady, with nothing but growing old on her mind!" Marion and Amy burst into giggles at the thought.

"She must be a real caution to that little group of positive thinkers she has in Bethany, "Amy shook her head. "Kind and patient with us all, but never seems to forget that, according to Proverbs "Life and death are in the power of the tongue."

Marion nodded. "And listen to me, planning other people's future, while my own is still in disarray. Well, not in complete disarray, actually. Guyus, or no, I should say *Judge* Guyus (the only thing missing was the robe) stopped off yesterday with a large, new, and very intimidating ledger under his arm and a very determined look in his eye. Honestly, I could feel the Internal Revenue Inquisition coming on. 'Early Christians' and I have a lot in common!"

"'If you are serious about this herb business'," he began, and I got a definite impression that he had a lot of doubt in that area, "I suggest that you begin immediately to keep an accurate inventory of all your merchandise, expenditures, etc. Not next year at tax time remember!'"

"Well I thanked him for the book. A handsome leather outfit that I guess some grateful client had given him. A lot more expensive than I would have purchased on my own, that's for sure."

"Didn't your bookkeeping notebooks last year come form the Emporium?" Amy teased.

"And from Pen's cut rate table," Marion admitted.

Pulling her housecoat more securely about her, Amy rose, reluctantly, to leave the comfort of Marion's kitchen for the steaming world outside.

"With Guyus to discipline our finances and health problems, and Crum to manage our daily lives we have it made, don't we". she laughed.

Chapter 22

AN IMPORTANT EVENT

Richard O. Ivy's marriage to Miss Geraldine Phipps might not be world shaking news anywhere else; it would make a back page in some nearby city since he owns the local newspaper, but it certainly made headlines in our *'Morning Sun'*

Not that Liberty Corners needed the printed notice. Trinity B. caught sight of them arriving, together, in a Bethany Taxi, apparently straight from the airport. It was early and she was finishing her second walk with the AWG's, just turning down Old McKinney Road. And there was Richard handing Miss Geraldine from the cab, with what Trin called such "tender solicitude". (any show of emotions sets Trinity's imagination ablaze.) Trin hesitated long enough to see Richard ordering the cabby to carry mounds of luggage up to the Mansion's ornate, newly refurbished door. Trin was convinced it was all the luggage, not just his own, and it was **all** being carried <u>inside</u> <u>the</u> <u>house</u> <u>together</u>. Well!

When she reached home Trin was still so excited Gert couldn't make head nor tail of what she was chattering about. However, a call from Marion, the Mansion's next door neighbor, verified the arrival within minutes and the whole village was aware before lunch. Later we were told the whole story.

According to Miss Geraldine, (pardon, Mrs. Richard 0. Ivy!) Richard had become uneasy about her decision to visit her sister before she agreed to his plans for an immediate ceremony. While she did agree to marry him, she had not set an exact date. He was afraid that either *she* might waver, or that her sister and brother in law might convince her to reconsider. At any rate, determination on high, he had invited himself to meet Vi and Victor and plead his case.

While Vi may have had some small reservations about her kindly, unprepossessing sister under the dominion of a man she had heard called "Richard the lion hearted," a few days of relaxed ambience in almost tropical sunshine had brought about an amazing euphoria.

Even Vi's dog 'Silas' had changed his attitude to this newcomer. From small but shrill warfarc carried on at ankle level (Richard aware that threads were being pulled from his trouser leg with each attempted bite) Silas, the owner of an truly dense coat of blond fur, had deposited himself on Richard's navy blue clad lap, and refused to be coaxed away. Vi, the dog lover, was delighted with this "Official seal of approval." Richard bore the whole episode with amazing grace.

It took only a few days of friendly family talk between Richard and his hosts before the idea of a small home wedding ceremony was introduced. Introduced by Richard and seconded with enthusiasm by Victor. Geraldine, complimented by the attention, and yet discomfited, offered many reasons for delay; all immediately discounted by first Richard, and then Victor and Vi. Victor himself made all the necessary arrangements with his own Pastor; Vi ordered flowers, between hugs and advice, and tears and more advice and...

Two wonderful weeks on Catalina Island followed, with Geraldine (at her own admission) reduced to happy tears many times at Richards solicitous attentions.

****

We have now received an official invitation. We are all to be the guests of Mr. and Mrs. Richard Ivy at the Mansion, for what we are telling ourselves is an "Open House" and informal reception for the bride and groom. Which may satisfy our enormous interest, not admitted as blatant curiosity, in the renovation of our only genuine local 'castle,' and allow us all to share the obvious joy of Richard and Geraldine.

That 'all' may include practically every Cornerite in the Village. In his sixty five years Richard has assumed the guise of corporate legacy; including the where-with-all for football uniforms that the school budget couldn't cover; the Library extension; the open checkbook when the 'Do' runs out of funds, etc. Sometimes Richard, the obdurate, appears a blessing in disguise on our 'cranky' days, or when he makes arbitrary decisions counter to Hazel Bernie's known opinions, but he and his generosity are there.

This invitation, I am honest enough to admit, we have all been waiting for since the day the remodeling began. Even while it was simply Richard's home, but even more so with the joyful news of the wedding. That 'no gifts' was a stipulation made loud and clear by Richard and echoed by Geraldine we know, but there will be exceptions; Gert has already framed a lovely water color that Geraldine admired at her last showing; Lila Mae Bernie has compiled an album of pictures, *finds* of the Ivy Family from a hundred years back garnered while she searched for Arthur Grigsby's museum artifacts; and Clemmy Lukes has every intention of presenting Geraldine with the Wedding Ring quilt that she has been working on for over a year.

For the present the rest of us will have to be satisfied with expensive cards from Stones Drug Store, with some practical gift later, or plants from Ebert Grant's green house. He has branched out into some strange, exotic flowers. So, we will not go empty handed to celebrate this important event.

****

Saturday, six P.M. in Liberty Corners

"Oh Gram, please... I know Mr. Ivy would want me to come to his party. Oh I just know he would." Charlie moved even closer against Marion's shoulder, his voice rose higher and higher and gathered more urgency.

"I know Mr. Ivy would want me to come Gram. I want to tell him about all the funny things that happened to the Beazley's working on his house when Mr. Ivy wasn't around. Legs and I watched all the time Gram. We even saw the day Goochie Beazley fell off the ladder and broke the new chandelier." Charlie paused for a moment to grin, lost in wonder at the remembered incident.

"His Daddy was so mad at him Gram he hit Goochie with that long pole he uses on the ceilings. Knocked him clear off the ladder again!"

Marion, seated before the only mirror in the house that didn't magnify the unkind shadows under her eyes, and apparently unsympathetic to the gravity of the situation, continued to brush her hair into its usual curly nothing. She was just about to apply rouge, Princess Pink, or rose... when his words finally penetrated. She straightened with a jerk.

"Charlie, oh Charlie, what are you saying? Don't you dare tell Richard any such a tale. The chandelier was broken in the shipping. Mr. Beazley told Richard all about it. It was just that delay in the new shipment that upset Richard so. My word, you certainly are not invited to the Open House, and don't you repeat this nonsense to anyone, hear?"

A few minutes later Marion, a small disturbing sense of guilt assailing, watched as Charlie, his last hope of joining the adults in what sounded like an exciting night, with wonderful treats delivered from Minton's famous Party House Restaurant, slipped an apple from a loaded basket on the hall table and plodded toward his bedroom. Resignation and defeat equally visible.

Marion stepped into the new blue dress, bought especially for the occasion at the "Miss Sophisticate" dress shop in Bethany, and jostled home in a large box aboard the Trailways Bus. Her expectations of a thoroughly pleasant evening just a little marred.

****

Lila Mae Bernie was busy. Both hands thrusting, no, not thrusting, Mama did not take to uneven treatment, 'easing' the elderly beige lace dress over Hazel's equally elderly shoulders.

"Hold still Mama, hold real still. I don't want to rip this old thing. Don't know why you're so set on wearing it. You could have a new dress."

Hazels voice rose to the challenge instantly. "It's my very best dress Lila Mae, real imported English lace, and only worn a half dozen times. Bought for me by your own Daddy when we had our open house right here on Edward Graham Road."

She hesitated. Lila Mae had called it "this old thing," was it really that many years since she had dressed for the opening of her own new home? Her usually positive manner took on a rather strange shade of uncertainty.

"Is it really too old fashioned, do you think? Isn't it fit? I want to do the right thing by Richard you know, long as I've known that family." She searched Lila Mae's face for confirmation.

"Ah, Mama, don't pay any attention to me, I'm just edgy. You'll do just fine. I just want to be sure we're ready when Gert comes to pick us up." A glance at her mothers face and she added, "Daddy surely knew what he was doing when he bought lace for you, and this color—a real lady's dress."

****

Her own rose jumper, featured in the latest catalog at a price she couldn't resist, has brought a lovely flush of excitement to her face. Enhanced at the last minute, and against her will, by Gert's application of a dusting of rose on each cheek. "Come on Lila Mae, it's a party, and Richard and Geraldine are so happy! Besides, we are to get our first view of how the other half lives, right?"

Chapter 23
THE EVENING

Richards affability during the entire evening is so pronounced that even Judge Guyus has had to take notice. After years of congenial, undeclared warfare; on every issue, from what new parking signs should be painted in the Square, to who should write the latest diatribe to the County. Getting used to the new Richard Ivy could prove unsettling.

Noel, a cup of coffee in hand and a proud eye focused on Cordy, is simply enjoying everything. Cordelia couldn't look prettier, in a dramatic wine caftan with Yetta's elegant silver ear drops, borrowed for the occasion, as she accepts goodies from the tray being passed among us repeatedly. The mouth watering goodies that Charlie had only guessed at, and coveted, as he watched the catering truck unload earlier. With any luck someone will remember tomorrow to send leftovers next door to Dracula's best friend, he hopes.

Garaldine's happiness is clear. That she actually welcomes Richard's encompassing devotion is apparent, and all the references to her superior talents in the redecorating project has brought an attractive blush to her unvarnished face. Urged on by our rampant curiosity Geraldine has taken us from room to room as we "oh" and "ah" at the improvements. The old 'detached' Richard has lost ground. Again and again he returns to Geraldine's side to offer a supporting elbow, and share the public's approbation, which he has always despised.

****

Hazel Bernie has had a glass of elderberry wine, against Lila's judgment, and is feeling no pain. After several compliments Hazel has given herself over to pure pleasure. Clemmy Lukes, the fabric queen, wedged herself in beside Hazel on the couch to examine and exclaim over the English lace; and Marion Lozier was noticeably impressed with the up swept hair do Lila managed with her Mama's rather scanty locks. In the excitement of the festivities she was even able to shake hands with Dr. Angus in a civilized manner, before she was quite aware of who she was greeting, that is. That she then turned abruptly to speak to another, he appreciated with a knowing laugh.

Lila Mae watched with favor as Marcus Curry accepted a small glass being urged on him by Ebert Grant. While Marcus is aware that wine was the accepted drink during our Lord's stay on earth (was water even readily available in desert country?) he is still wary of overdoing anything in 'the name of the Lord.' The wonderful cheese tarts are a different matter however, no urging necessary.

Chapter 23
THE FOLLOWING DAY

The oversize and clearly numbered clock on the Emporium wall struck seven as Albert set about opening his market. Albert had the numerals hand painted on a large octagon shaped clock face when he discovered many of us peering up at the old clock and then questioning the veracity of our findings.

As he pulled the heavy shades at the front window he winced. Have to check those cords, getting to show their age; fraying and making strange squeaks each morning as they were raised, and even worse when lowered nightly. He glanced into the Square just in time to see busy, methodical Ebert Grant, his truck loaded to the top of it's boarded sides with fall bounty, headed for the market in Minton. Albert gave a cheerful wave; his share of Grants Farm produce would be delivered at his own loading platform out back, by noon.

Ebert merely nodded, eyes intent on avoiding a collision with Grigsby's rather dusty Cadillac. He grinned as he watched Darling Mauveleen performing her "I hate the world" ritual dance in the rear window of Lilly's car. Feisty little beggar. Did pets and owners really share the same personality? She was Lily's dog. Arthur now, always seemed to be a cheerful kind of laid back individual. The very kind that would drive his own purposeful,'get it done yesterday' wife Amy up the wall, he realized. He pulled around carefully; twenty five minutes to reach Minton Market and then back for a load of fresh corn to Bethany.

Albert watched as Lilly urged a reluctant Pekingese into a carrying basket and entered the store.

"Morning Lilly, wonderful day."

Armed with her bouncing, jostling burden, (Darling Mauveleen resents confinement), Lily gave a distracted greeting and moved toward the meat counter. "Not too bad for this time of year Albert. Not quite cool enough yet though. Not like we usually enjoy in the Corners." Her tone spoke it's usual frustration.

"It'll change fast enough. Always fools us into believing we're going to have a second summer, then wham, we're searching the closet for that sweater we donated to the Goodwill last spring. Now, what are we needing this morning Lilly? Have some nice fresh liver for Mauvaleen of course, and a really great New York steak I'm saving for Arthur." Albert's good humor is almost foolproof against all our moods.

"The liver sounds fine Albert. My poor darling's appetite has been all at sixes and sevens lately." Lilly patted the carryall affectionately. "I'll let Arthur come over and choose dinner for himself, if he ever decides to get up, that is. Sound asleep when I left the house. After only two glasses of Richard's champagne last night he was in such a wonderful humor he insisted he would be at the Mansion by eight his morning to help Richard move that big cabinet Geraldine says she wants in the pantry." Lilly shook her head in wonder." Imagine; a freshly painted butlers pantry... shelves on three walls, and still room for a cabinet!"

Albert grinned. "Seeing that house is going to cause a lot of dissatisfaction in the village. Every woman in town determined to remodel, especially her kitchen. Pen has already decided to call the Beazleys to see what we can do about ours. The party was fun though, wasn't it? Good food, good drinks. Everybody relaxed and in good spirits."

"Yes, good to see Richard happy and relaxed for a change. Always seems to be up tight about something, especially if Dicky boy shows up." Lilly's voice dripped with disapproval.

"Yeh, he was in a good mood wasn't he? Well maybe Geraldine is the answer to too many lonely hours and no close family relationship."

Albert wrapped the generous supply of liver carefully, and followed Lilly to the door, keeping all fingers a cautious distance from Darling Mauveleen's active wire enclosure. Arthur would have to fend for himself.

****

A lingering, stretched expanse of Sunday sun streamed in the long window; exposing a peaceful, tranquil oasis two stories above the street level. Dr Angus Steele's office over looking the Square.

Angus, settled in his worn chair, allowed himself one of those rare moments of complete satisfaction; being in the right place, at the right time, doing work he loved. Gratification, for what amounted to an established practice, (most of the patients he saw had been under Dr. Christian's care, or were the children of those who had been) good people, reasonable people. Now one more potential problem laid to rest. Richard Ivy, his special friend, under the benevolent dominion of Geraldine Phipps might be able to get his priorities under control. And so far, there was no word from Dicky, at least not in his hearing.

Great party. Richard so busy being gracious to all of us he had no time to eat, or better yet, drink. Accepting that beautiful and serene landscape from Gert Ealy in front of us all was just the right touch. Gave everyone a chance to be a small part of the Mansion redecorating. Geraldine's idea he was sure.

He must get Ruth to think of some special gift they could give the Ivy's. Women were better at these things. And, how come he didn't have one of Gert's paintings right here in his office?

Chapter 24
REACTIONS

There is a definite change at Liberty Library. But it's only temporary, the former Miss Geraldine has assured everyone. While Richard will probably prefer a full time, homebody wife, and the wonderful new kitchen presents a strong temptation to abandon books in favor of recipes, it's no easy thing to walk away from a work you have loved for over twenty years.

So, there was some waiting at the front desk this morning when the Library opened. None of the usual immediate 'strictly for business' service. With the sometimes austere eye of Miss Geraldine missing, Cordelia is holding relaxed court with two teen aged aids in attendance. Martin Grant, creative juices on high since the recent publication of his own 'dog' story, has placed several volumes on writing in front of Cordelia; he would love to discuss the authors.

Trinity, booksack slung over her shoulder, takes the opportunity to study every detail of Cordelia's hair style; the cut of the new tan jumper; the clipped, unpainted fingernails. So pretty, and engaged to be married! How can she still look so calm and sort of detached? Romantic notions rampant, Trin, the willing victim of every Hollywood male sensation appearing weekly at the State Theater, shook her head in wonder. How could she dare to keep that darling Professor dangling? The way he looked at her even as they shopped at the market gave Trin goose bumps.

Cordelia, marking each card, placed it in the corresponding book for Martin and turned to her next patron and smiled.

"Hi Trin, how are you doing? Having any trouble keeping up with the 'AWG'S? Haven't overslept and brought a reprimand down on your head, I hope."

Trin laughed. “Not so far. Had to run all across town to catch up last Monday though. Tom left on time, but I was on the phone with Gloria, and Flinders was in one of his bratty moods.”

“That’s quite a cat, according to all I hear. Siamese, isn’t it?”

“Worse,” Trin giggled,” Flinders is Balinese. Gert says he’s really too high and mighty for our house. Royalty, being entertained in an unworthy way, by peasants... We’ve had special trouble ever since Tom was forced to sprinkle a vitamin on Flin’s favorite canned duck.”

Pride and irritation mixed equally as she continued. “Any rational method of medicating that cat spells disaster! Flinders is convinced that his life is in jeopardy. We are all under suspicion.” At this point Trinity and Cordelia’s laughter has brought the teen aids up close to the desk to enjoy the joke.

“The way he crawls up to his food bowl - - - -! He stops short by at least a foot and begins to sniff. If he’s not completely satisfied he circles the bowl and then flattens on the linoleum in a disgusting, spastic way, to meditate, before he’ll even taste it. You can just hear him thinking, ‘Have they laced this with arsenic? Watson to the rescue!’”

Still smiling, Trinity packed her new romance novels into the back pack and took off for home and a fresh confrontation with a wily beast.

****

While the County Board has not had an official notice of a possible vacancy in the staff at Liberty Library (Richard’s permission to share his wife’s time with the rest of us still in question) two of the members of the Board were invited to drink champagne and crunch delectables at the party with the rest of Liberty Corners. We all offered our valuable advice of course.

Tentative suggestions were made during the evening; mention was made of one John Clancy, a recent graduate of Liberty College, as a possible replacement for whatever opening occurs. Grand nephew to the late Mr. Worley. Which is all in his favor, we do tend to promote 'our own.' Tall, blond, with scholarly good looks, and, affable; at variance with his cantankerous great Uncle. He would probably meet with our approval, especially the feminine gender at Liberty High. And we think he may have been mentioned in the will, so the small salary involved is not critical. The county is not noted for overpaying it's workers.

****

Noel, enthusiasm on high, swooped up to the curbside and pressed the horn, just as Cordelia left the Library at the noonday break.

"Perfect timing, I thought you might like to check the property again." Clutching her hand he drew her into the car and held her tight against him for one quick moment. "Cordy, Cordy".

Cordelia laughed and, very gently pushed free. "Noel, please, the Volunteers knew when you called, and they were lined up at the window before I got my purse out of the desk. They didn't want to miss a thing."

"Let them look... Oh I love you Cordy dear, when are you going to marry me?" His voice and manner begged for an answer.

She lifted his hand and held it against her cheek "Soon darling Noel, very soon." With only a note of reproach, she reminded him "Remember, we're all that Yetta and Guyus have... Now that I know that Guyus approves..."

Fingers caressed Cordelia's cheek lightly "Approves isn't the word, he's impatient now, you'd think it was a court case that he wants settled." Cordelia nodded, "Now I want Yetta to be happy too."

****

"You all right Mama?" Lila Mae, the caretaker, stared at her mother anxiously. Mama has been extra quiet all day. Hadn't even seemed to notice the wonder working fall weather washing over Liberty Corners. Clear benevolent warmth. Summer refusing, with gentle determination, to give up her rights. Refusing to move aside for a robust, sometimes unruly September.

Hazel, boredom and martyrdom equally divided settled in her wheel chair, a shawl and the Ladies Aid quilt pushed to one side against the mounting heat, simply nodded assurance at Lila Mae.

"I'm fine Lila Mae. Just fine."

"Don't need anything? A glass of lemonade, or"

"No, Lila Mae. Thank you, but don't fuss Lila Mae."

Still not convinced Lila Mae shifted the chair an inch closer to the shady area and tucked the quilt more firmly under Hazel's unwilling elbow.

"Well then I'll go on with my work."

Aware, distracted, and just a little irritated by Lila Mae's obvious concern Hazel reached to give Lila Mae's hand a gentle pat.

"I'm fine Lila Mae. Just thinking. Fall's a thinking time. Spring brings up a dozen interesting and exciting ideas, things to do, things to get accomplished, but September says it's done, too late to start again. At least for me. At eighty." Lila Mae smiled, Mama still hedging where actual years must be admitted.

Hazel sighed and then allowed herself a little half humorous, half apologetic laugh, "But mind you don't repeat any of this to Yetta Wiley. She'll be at the door signing me up for her Positive Thinking class. Probably knows a dozen projects I could start tomorrow. Writing my memoirs, a history of the Corners; even tried to get me interested in joining a pottery class down at the Art Center." She smiled. "That actually caught my attention. Even little Charlie found that exciting."

****

Yetta Wiley, Emporium's handy basket clutched under one arm, leaned against the corner of the meat counter and stared, uninterested, unseeing, at the row of fresh cod spread before her. Frozen codfish eyes stared back. She smiled to herself, 'You are about as concerned with me as I am with you...' Meanwhile from the corner of her eye she was observing the slow but deliberate progress of Guyus Carpentar in her direction. Entering from the back door, only used by the privileged few, past boxes of fresh produce that jammed the aisle. Each step measured carefully, to avoid worldly contact with his handsome jacket or trousered leg. Distinguished, unapproachable, and soon to be related to Henry's daughter, Cordelia. What had Henry thought of this man, Yetta wondered. Other than casual contact in the village, and the inevitable 'across the table' arguments at town meetings, she realized that she herself hardly knew the man. Had Henry ever taken any particular notice of the Carpentars? Not likely, Cordelia had never shown any interest in the son while Henry was living. Not that Yetta was aware of.

Reaching the counter, and wishing fervently that Beulah was here; (she always knew how to handle personal level contacts so much better; even embarrassed. him with her open friendliness, and accused him of being 'an old stick') Guyus smiled now and proffered a tentative hand.

"Good morning, good morning, Mrs. Wiley. And how are you? I trust you are as happy with what the future holds for our young people as I am?" Yetta raised her hand; clean unpolished fingers slid into the authoritative grasp of a manicured hand. "Good Morning Judge Carpentar. Yes indeed, yes indeed. They are both so happy." Judge Guyus considered the tall quiet woman; his son's future mother-in-law, and his future friend, or adversary? The first awkward words out of the way, Yetta Wiley, positive thinker, relaxed and prepared to enjoy Cordelia's new in-law.

Chapter 25
FINALLY

"All things working together for good" and to our satisfaction... The plans for the very quiet wedding of Noel and Cordelia is now set for the first week of October. That Cordelia's desire for a simple ceremony met with the Judge's approval was obvious; plain dealing Noel just wants whatever makes his 'Cordy' happy. In our almost daily contacts in the Village, Yetta Wiley continues to drift on in her usual kind but impersonal way, but we notice that the Judge has taken to mentioning his 'daughter' in his conversations in the waiting line at the Emporium lately. With rather warm approbation actually. Which is a good sign; they, (Noel and Cordy, with Guyus' fervent agreement) have decided to make their home with the Judge, temporarily, until Zenith Construction from Minton can begin work on 'Highpoint' their dream home. Already named, it's to occupy the pinnacle of their acreage, with a supreme view of the whole valley. The lovely elms will be left in place, and the house nestled in their center, if Noel has his way.

Marcus will officiate at the solemn rite, of course. In that same cheerful, sparkling, little church that witnessed the ostentatious wedding of Attorney Guyus Carpentar and Beulah Graham, the heiress, some thirty five years ago. But the similarity ends with the building; or is supposed to...if Cordelia's wishes are to be respected!

However... Guyus will feel obliged to invite one or two of his closest colleagues; and Barry Thornton, Noel's fellow Professor, must be included; which means that his close neighbor and associate, Miss Campbell from the College, and her Mama, would certainly be offended if overlooked. Cordelia's close association with Geraldine at the Library has developed into a warm friendship, and now there is Richard to be considered. (He has insisted on providing special transportation to and from the

Airport in Bethany for the two week honeymoon, to...destination unknown.) Yetta, determined that 'the children' be allowed to make their own plans; has merely suggested that the ladies from her 'Group' would love to attend the service. Village minded Marcus, would open the doors to all of us I'm sure, but hesitates to interfere.

****

Meantime Marion and Gert Ealy are enthusiastic about their plans for a lovely reception on the newlyweds return. Marion is pulling out all her best cook books, and Clemmy, with the 'special recipes' that Gramps declares God has bequeathed her, is anxious to introduce her delicious 'pumpkin treats.' I'm afraid the whole town expects, *and intends,* to be included in this. Charlie has already taken a stand.

"Gram", he offers at the breakfast table," Gram, you know Noel and I are friends." Here his voice takes on an unwarranted confidence," Almost best friends, really, 'cause of Dracula." Marion, busy with the latest list of 'things she must remember to get in Bethany' stops to stare at Charlie. "You're *best friends* with *who?"*

Slightly discomfited Charlie grins, "Well, he talks to me every day when he goes for his 'run' mornings. I help when Dracula gets in his way." His smile grew wider. "I told you Gram, Dracula won't mind Noel any better than me, and when Noel tries to pass without even stopping to pat him, ol' Dracula runs between Noel's legs so Noel *has* to stop. Almost trips him."

Trying to ignore Marion's skeptical look, and shaking his head at Dracula's impudence, Charlie placed another pat of butter on his waiting toast; he began to cover the edges, very carefully; he hated to bite into the crusts where Gram never got the edges covered.

"So, I believe Gram, I really believe," he stresses the word but Marion seems unimpressed, "I believe Noel would want me to be invited to his party." Marion winced slightly, remembering that she had had to deny poor little Charlie entrance to the Ivy's celebration. She will consider this request.

****

Hazel Bernie doesn't actually plan on attending Noel's wedding; Lila Mae will represent them; (she and Cordelia have developed a strange, rather humorous relationship, comparing sympathetic and affectionate notes on the entire Village, as they labored together at the Circle.) But that Hazel means to be a part of the reception she has made clear. The 'lady' dress has undergone one more careful pressing, (Lila Mae held her breath as the steam iron snatched at the lacy edges despite her lightest touch) and Mama has even asked Lila to 'do something about my hair' the day of the party. While Mintons 'Party House' is famous for specialities, and we enjoyed every bite at Ivy's reception, we don't know anyone who can surpass Marion's culinary skills. Clemmy will add her own edibles and Miss Bloome (from the Bank) is already counting calories so she can indulge without guilt.

Since Charlie is to be invited, (after all, it's to be held at *his* house), Clemmy must make up her mind whether her little charges should be included. Perhaps Emmy and Ben, not the two youngest? Everyone in town knows Noel of course, he has that kind of personality; and Cordelia has established herself with the children as the 'second library ogre.'

****

That Professor Carpentar's attention span right now is in a chaotic state; on any matter not directly connected with his upcoming wedding plans. We watched and enjoyed his acquiring of property for the first time, since we *knew* what that was leading to, so the present state was to be expected. Maybe some of his students, especially those he has been tutoring during the summer, have enjoyed his inattention to microscopic details (that has been an identifying mark in his teaching career) but there has been one casualty. Martin Grant, our 'wanna be' writer. It has come at a most inconvenient time too. After months of study on the intricacies of *'making your words count'* and the interest and support of Professor Carpenter, Martin finally submitted a story, entitled "The Free of Charge Puppy" to a national magazine, and the anxiety is unbearable.

This morning Martin Grant made slow progress up the path to the door of the parsonage. A lackadaisical hand pressed the buzzer, even as he looked through the great bay window at Pastor Marcus, seated at his desk, in plain view. Taking note of the downcast look Marcus raised a hand and motioned him in. Young people... so easily cast down, bless their hearts; what could have created such a 'catastrophe' this early in the day?

"Good morning Martin my boy, how are you this beautiful day," his hand reached out.

Martin, Alma Grant's disciplined son offered a hand and a rather constrained smile. "Morning Pastor. Is this a bad time to drop in, am I interrupting something?"

Marcus got up from the desk and settled hospitably on a small couch. "Not at all, this is perfect timing. I needed a visit; now tell me how the writing is going. Heard anything yet? When did you submit that good dog story?"

Marcus has been mentoring the literary talents of Noel Carpentar's budding author while Noel has been busy settling his own future. A kind and patient substitute for the English Professor, but Marcus has never gone through the awful pain associated with literary ambitions. Marcus has never published anything. In fact Marcus has never *written* anything, except his own sermons; and there has been no public clamor for copies.

A defeated look and a heavy sigh assures Marcus that he is asking the wrong question, or at least he is asking at the wrong time "It's been three months Pastor. The ad said the winners would be announced by September." He was treated to yet another sigh, then, "They probably got hundreds of submissions, probably didn't even read mine. I expect I'm just kidding myself."

"Now Martin," soft spoken Marcus can take issue with faith that wavers. "Now Martin, Didn't we ask for guidance on this?"

Martin nodded.

"And I'm sure you believed it was time to... at least try to get your story published. And now it's been three months...." Marcus studied young Martins expression sympathetically.

Then smiling affectionately he ventured quietly, "It would be interesting to know what questions, and yes, doubts, went through our father Abraham's mind while he waited, year after year, for *his* promised answer, wouldn't it."

Chapter 26
DECISIONS AGAIN

We like to see problems settled, to *our* satisfaction. *Other peoples problems,* that is. The 'concerns' of the whole Village that Gert Ealy has accused Marion of taking on herself. Now, with Richard and Geraldine settled in the Mansion; the lovely renovated Mansion, that can make most of us green with envy if we compare our 1930's kitchens to the beautiful mechanical marvel that they are enjoying; and Judge Carpenter, smug and satisfied with his new family connections; another 'case' settled to his satisfaction, another young person under his wise jurisdiction; we can all relax, and settle back. Nothing more to pique our interest or our curiosity. Miss Blaome, making her way through the bank this morning could be heard to murmur, "And how long will that last?"

Nothing except our 'project,' that is. Guyus is beginning to show definite signs of dissatisfaction when the 'Do' comes up in any conversation however. Which it always does. It is still the 'fun' activity that brings us all together. Most of the time in harmony, once the usual problems are settled; who gets what space at the Market House; what part the children from Edward Graham Elementary will play; where do we find someone to repair Joshua Luke's calliope, etc. etc.

Grampa Joshua Lukes found the calliope on the East Coast, in 1930. The thundering blast of sound and fury constituted the ultimate and exultant symbol of joy since his arrival in America a half century before. A circus, fallen into financial problems, offered the opportunity to *own* the magic gold pipes. It was too much! Middle aged Joshua literally thrust money (that he needed urgently for other purposes) into the hands of the circus owner; hauled his prize across miles of highway, to be established, a royal queen on a concrete dais, in his own barn. Where it sits, protected with a heavy tarp against dust and changing weather, and only exposed to the reverential eyes of Gramps and his grandchildren on special occasions. Until that important first week of December... That Ebert Grant, a sometimes musician, could play the thing, was Gramp's final proof of God's benevolence.

While obdurate may be the word applied secretly to Richard Ivy, Judge Guyus is recognized as the original 'Organizer.' And it's only honest to admit that as the year end looms, his is the one imposing figure that we hope to avoid at the Emporium, and First Christian, and even at Interstate Bank. And in a town the size of the Corners where do you hide when you see him heading your way, a solemn court room judgement on his still handsome face?

That his agitation about this matter is serious we are aware. Several ambitious business entrepreneurs from upstate have had their eye on our project, and would like to have a piece of the pie. They have money they are anxious to invest, and hope that there is someone in Liberty Corners with an itchy palm. They have approached Richard, and Tom Ealy (from the Real Estate angle) without success, and Guyus' attitude doesn't encourage any outside participation in our strictly non-profit, old fashioned friendship, venture. Other than convincing Marcus Severns that including 'outsiders' could be a *soul winning strategy,* their efforts will be fruitless against our original posture. A little friendly pride in our own way of life, *and the fear of losing it;;* could that be the name of the game?

****

The evening suns last rays fell in a witching time pattern across Dr, Angus' desk. Lackluster fall sunshine, softer, less pervasive, after two months of gleeful near tyranny that wrapped all Corners ladies in confusion; "what should I wear today, is it sandals and a sundress or can I dare to try the new two piecer I bought especially for fall?" That Angus is spared any trauma on dress is obvious. His uniform has just been changed, for *another of the same.* (Kursty Lukes, after only two ice creams, followed by a wild water battle in Marion's Super Cyclone pool managed to lose all as Angus tried to check her tonsils. Clemmy, picking her up at Marion's and knowing nothing of the treats, had brought her to Dr. Angus as a precaution when she complained of "cramps in her middle.")

Leaning past his computer, Angus is focusing on an almost deserted Square. Silent, shadow ridden, four blocks of familiar brick; with an unknown, show room new car pulling into a parking space immediately beneath his window. Who in Liberty Corners has been hoarding their tax refund long enough to afford what is obviously an 'Auto Lane" special from Minton? A nicely dressed young man gets out of the drivers seat, looks about with what appears to be friendly familiarity, and makes his way to Stones Drug Store. Angus, one hand raised to his forehead, shades his tired eyes in an effort to guarantee that he is seeing what his weary mind says he is seeing, but is refusing to accept. With a humorous murmur he settled back in his chair... Nothing is impossible... And almost two years have passed since his last personal appearance. Perhaps young Ivy has gotten his act together.

****

www.ingramcontent.com/pod-product-compliance
Ingram Content Group UK Ltd.
Pitfield, Milton Keynes, MK11 3LW, UK
UKHW040016200726
13854UKWH00001B/240

9 780759 626133